Queering SF

Queering SF: Readings

by
Ritch Calvin

Aqueduct Press
PO Box 95787
Seattle, Washington 98145-2787
www.aqueductpress.com

Copyright © 2022 Ritch Calvin
All rights reserved

Library of Congress Control Number: 2021952812

ISBN: 978-1-61976-220-6
First Edition, First Printing, May 2022

Cover Illustration: ESA/Hubble & NASA, Z. Levay

Book and cover design by Kathryn Wilham

Acknowledgments

I would like to acknowledge the support of the Dean of the College of Arts and Sciences. That support made the completion of this book far easier.

I would also like to acknowledge the keen eyes, insight, and knowledge of Timmi Duchamp and Kath Wilham. Their support and attention to detail made this book far better than it would have been.

I would like to acknowledge Mary Jo Bona for her friendship and support. Her support has made me a better scholar and a better person.

*Dedication
to all my students,
who continue to inspire me
to teach and to learn*

Contents

36 Shades of Queer: An Introduction 1

1. It's My Body, and I'll Try If I Want To
   (John Varley's "Options") 5
2. Swastikas Tonight
   (Katherine Burdekin's *Swastika Night*) 15
3. Sex and/or Dangerous Visions
   (Samuel R. Delaney's "Aye…and Gomorrah" and
   Carol Emshwiller's "Sex and/or Mr. Morrison") 21
4. Listening to the Female Man
   (Joanna Russ's *The Female Man*) 27
5. A Body of Excess
   (Tanith Lee's *Don't Bite the Sun*) 35
6. Queer Families and Queer Gender
   (Alan Brennert's "The Third Sex," Raphael Carter's
   "The Congenital Agenesis of Gender Ideation,"
   Gwyneth Jones's "La Cenerentola,"
   and James Patrick Kelly's "Lovestory") 45
7. Queering Sex, Love, and SF
   (Larissa Lai's *Salt Fish Girl*) 53
8. Sex without Bodies
   (Caitlin Sullivan and Kate Bornstein's
   Nearly Roadkill) 59
9. Binary Queer
   (Jennifer Marie Brissett's *Elysium*) 65
10. Digital Memorials
    (Gabriela Damián Miravete's
    "And They Will Dream in the Garden") 71

i

11. Hermaphrodites in Space
    (Sayuri Ueda's *The Cage of Zeus*) 75
12. Janelle Monáe's Queer America
    (Janelle Monáe's *Dirty Computer*) 81
13. *Sense8*, Queering the Family, and the Collective
    (The Wachowski's *Sense8*) 85
14. A Bridge Cemented in Blood
    (Ursula K. Le Guin's *The Left Hand of Darkness*) 89
15. Queer Muslims in Space
    (Amal El Mohtar's "To Follow the Waves" and
    An Owomoyela's "A God in the Sky") 95
16. Recentering Life in *Salt Fish Girl*
    (Larissa Lai's *Salt Fish Girl*) 99
17. What's YOUR Superpower?
    (Su J. Sokol's "Je me souviens") 103
18. Queer Love in the Time of Pandemic
    (Tristan Alice Nieto's "Imago") 107
19. Love and Sex at the End of the Earth
    (N. K. Jemisin's *The Fifth Season*) 111
20. "Bloodchild" and the Queer Family
    (Octavia E. Butler's "Bloodchild") 117
21. Aliens and Drag Queens in "The Moon Room"
    (Maria Romasco Moore's "The Moon Room") 121
22. *Bitch Planet*? "You're Already on It"
    (Kelly Sue DeConnick's *Bitch Planet*) 125
23. Karel Čapek, Robots, and Queer Family
    (Blue Dellaquanti's *O Human Star*) 129
24. Queer Family in Ohio
    (Brendan Williams-Childs's "Schwaberow, Ohio") .. 133

25. Trans Time Travel
    (Nino Cipri's "The Shape of My Name") 137
26. The Heat Death of the Individual
    (M. Téllez's "The Heat Death
    of Human Arrogance") 141
27. How Many Is Too Few?
    (A. E. Prevost's "Sandals Full of Rainwater") 145
28. From the Space of Compassion
    (Merc Fenn Wolfmoor's
    "The Frequency of Compassion") 149
29. The Heretic Has Left the Building
    (Ada Hoffman's "Minor Heresies") 153
30. Asexual Self-Love
    (Sarah Kanning's "Sex with Ghost") 157
31. It Gets Better, Even in Kansas
    (Nino Cipri's "Ad Astra Per Aspera") 161
32. Breaking the Binary
    (Cynthia Ward's "Body Drift") 165
33. The Age of Destruction
    (Merc Fenn Wolfmoor's "The Lawless") 171
34. A Literal Metaphor
    (Isabel Fall's "I Sexually Identify
    As an Attack Helicopter") 175
35. Swedish Retail Therapy
    (Nino Cipri's *Finna*) 181
36. Who You Looking At?, or How YA SF
    Became Intersectional
    (Alechia Dow's *The Sound of Stars*) 187

Primary Works Cited 191
Secondary Works Cited 196

36 Shades of Queer: An Introduction

WHAT IS SF? Well, that's the question. The answers are as varied as the people you ask. Their answers have filled volumes, from the practical to the esoteric, from the sublime to the ridiculous. I tend to use self-identification as a rule of thumb. If an author identifies their text as SF (science fiction or speculative fiction), then I accept that. That leads to the question, though, why do *they* consider it SF? In what ways does the piece conform to, or push at the boundaries of, what is generally accepted as SF?

What does SF do? Yes, it imagines new technologies. Yes, it imagines other worlds or societies. But at its very best, it asks questions. It compels the reader to ask questions. It makes the reader see something in a new light. It asks the reader to consider the verities of this world and to wonder if they might be mistaken. Maybe it gets us all to think about the world just a little bit queerly.

So, what is "queer"? Another very large question. At various times, the term means (or has meant) an insult, an identity, a set of practices, or an interpretive framework. For our purposes here, it means the last three of those definitions.

What does queer—and queer theory—have to do with SF? The queer theorist William Haver (he/him) has wondered about this. Haver writes about "queer" as "making strange, queer, or even cruel what we had thought to be a world" (in Golding, 1997, 291). In other words, the queer also asks us to consider the world as we know it just a little bit queerly.

1

In this sense, SF and queer are asking the reader to do similar things.

In terms of queer SF, the year 2010 seems to have been a watershed year. For whatever set of reasons, the number of queer SF texts exploded. The reasons included the following: changes in society, including the same-sex marriage debates; changes in social media gender/sexuality protocols; debates around "don't ask, don't tell"; coming of age of Gen Xers and Gen Yers; new people in editorial and publishing positions; dramatic shifts in publishing outlets and platforms. In 2020, Lee Mandelo (he/they) convened a virtual roundtable of writers of queer SF to ask about the changes in the past decade. According to these writers, a lot has changed, but it's not enough. The field *has* changed, but it's not where it needs to be.

We can all probably name queer texts that came before: the proto-queer texts, the historical queer texts, the subtle or coded queer texts (read Wendy Gay Pearson's she/her] essay, "Alien Cryptographies" for more on this). But explicit queer SF texts filled with queer characters and queer frameworks perhaps not so much.

Even with the increased number of explicitly queer SF texts, heteronormative privilege dominates SF publishing. One sign of privilege is if an author/text does not carry the entire weight of a marginalized community. For example, a cis-het, white writer can write an awful book, replete with racism, sexism, and homophobia, and that book will not reflect badly on cis-het, white writers. No one will say, "You see. I told you they were bad." No, no one will say, "You see, that reflects badly on the cis-het white community." Or, no one will say, "That just does not reflect the reality of cis-het lives." No, it can stand on its own.

The same cannot be said for queer writers of SF. Every character they write, every world they build, every text they publish will reflect on queer writers, queer communities, and queer SF. (See the discussion below on "I Sexually Identify As an Attack Helicopter.")

Perhaps more important than the sheer number of queer writers of SF is that fact that queer writers of SF continue to shape the *entire* field, sad puppies notwithstanding. Queer writers of SF demand better management and publishing practices; queer writers of SF develop new outlets; queer writers of SF offer texts that live up to the promise of a differently imagined future. What good is shiny new technology and colonies in space if we're stuck in the same old social and political patterns of marginalization, discrimination, and exploitation? What good is genetic modification and disease eradication if only the same groups of people benefit? What good is longevity (even immortality) if the society is a nightmare (see discussion below of Janelle Monáe).

What I hope to do in the following essays is (1) to introduce readers to some of the shades of queer in SF writing. SF is not a monolith. Queer SF is not, either. Writers of queer SF approach it in a variety of ways, with a variety of end goals. I also hope (2) to introduce some writers and texts that readers may not know about. As I noted, the field has opened up, and it is no longer easy to keep up with. In addition, I hope (3) to demonstrate some of the ways in which queer SF pushes at the very generic norms of SF. The idea of SF, the characteristics of SF, the content of SF have all been shaped (a) in a particular place and time, and (b) in your own reading experience. Many of these writers want to challenge what SF looks like and does. And finally, I hope (4) to point to some of these newly imagined futures, to spend some time in differently imagined societies and families, and to think about the ways in which you would like to see that in our own reality.

The genesis of this book lies in teaching. I have taught several courses on Queer SF in the past few years (2019-21). Nothing builds a knowledge base like prepping new courses. I read far and wide in order to put together the syllabi. Further, nothing makes one think through a text like preparing to teach it. As a way of preparing to teach each of the following texts (stories, novels, graphic novels, albums), I would write a draft of an essay, setting out the key issues for discussion of the texts (author bio, historical background, literary connections) and ways in which the texts operate as queer SF. In this sense, the following essays are fleshed-out outlines for teaching the texts.

Finally, the essays that follow are only a beginning. Although the trickle has begun, the real cascade has yet to appear. I can't wait to teach new courses on Queer SF. I can't wait to see what the next ten years of Queer SF brings. As Richard Labonté (he/him) and Lawrence Schimel (he/him) wrote in their 2006 anthology, *The Future Is Queer*.

A note on pronouns: I have tried to the best of my ability to locate the pronouns for people discussed in the book. I have consulted home pages, references pages, publisher pages, and social media to determine what pronouns a person uses. However, I am aware that, sometimes, the internet does not get things correct. I am also aware that pronouns are not fixed and stable and that they change over time. The pronouns used in mid-2021 may be different in late-2021 or 2050. Nevertheless, I believe that it is important to used desired pronouns whenever possible: (a) it acknowledges the individuals themselves, and (b) it is consistent with the aim and message of the book.

A note on spoilers: A number of the following readings will contain spoilers. I have tried to minimize these instances; however, a few spoilers remain. Reader beware.

1. It's My Body, and I'll Try If I Want To...

Take a trip back with father Tiresias
Listen to the old one speak of all he has lived through
"I have crossed between the poles, and for me there is no mystery
Once a man, like the sea I raged
Once a woman, like the Earth I gave...."

—Genesis, "The Cinema Show"

THE FASCINATION WITH sex is old; the fascination with the experience of other sexes is also quite old. In his *Metamorphoses*, Ovid (he/him) writes of the seer Tiresias. He had been called in to settle a dispute between Zeus and Hera about which sex enjoys the act of sex more. They called on Tiresias to settle this dispute because he had been transformed into a woman years earlier when he separated two mating snakes. So, because Tiresias had lived as both male and female, Zeus and Hera thought he would be ideal to answer the question.

John Varley's (he/him) semi-canonical story, "Options," reimagines the myth of Tiresias for a technological age. The novelette first appeared in 1979 in Terry Carr's (he/him) *Universe 9* collection. Varley himself has led an interesting and itinerant life. According to his own webpage, he fled his homeland of Texas for a college scholarship in Michigan, but he found academia boring. He dropped out, became a hippie, and lived in San Francisco for a while. After a period of years struggling to support himself financially, he decided in 1973 to write science fiction, and he has written ever since. While he is well-known for his Geaen trilogy and his Thunder and Lighting series of novels, it was "Persistence of Vision" (1978) that put him on the map. Over the course of his career, his work has garnered 9 Locus Awards, 3 Hugo Awards, 2 Nebula Awards, and 1 each of the Analog Award and the Apollo Award.

So, early in his career, and just six years after he started writing, he published "Options."

This updated version of the Tiresias myth is set in an undetermined future in King City on the moon and centers on a single family: Cleopatra, Jules, Lilli, Paul, and Feather. Cleo (she/her) is an architect and Jules (he/him) works in an unnamed business. While both are professionals, much of the domestic and care work falls on Cleo. In other words, gender roles have remained largely intact. And, yet, other social mores have changed. Public nudity seems to be a non-issue, as many of the poorer residents cannot afford the disposable clothing, and their children attend school naked. Open relationships seem to be a norm, as well. Both Jules and Cleo have lovers outside the marriage, typically with the knowledge and consent of their partner.

And, yet, Cleo struggles with three children at breakfast while Jules calmly reads the morning news (on an iPad-like device). After every one has been dealt with, Cleo herself heads to work, taking Feather with her because the baby is still breastfeeding. The commute is long for Cleo, as they had decided to live nearer to Jules's work. As Feather breastfeeds while they commute, Cleo reads the news on her own newsreader, including a story about the rise of "changers"—those who undergo sex confirmation surgery. At this time, science and technology have made sex changes quick and easy. Essentially, they grow a clone of someone's body in a mere six months and then transplant the brain, intact, in a simple procedure. The patient walks out an hour later.

The technology, from the vantage of 2021, seems a bit farfetched. That, I would argue, is not the point. Varley is not really concerned with whether or not our technology will get there one day—though it just *might*. He's not engaged in technological extrapolation, but rather sociological extrapolation. His real concern here is with examining sex, gender, and sexuality and their relation to the body.

Cleo finds herself just not feeling satisfied. She loves being a woman. She loves being a mother (even if at times she wishes differently). She loves having sex with her husband (even if she sometimes wishes it were not always on his terms). And, yet, something is missing. And so she's intrigued by the notion of changing sexes. Later, Cleo mentions "Changers" to Jules, but he resists. He has no interest in changing, and he hopes she doesn't, either. Jules finds it "a little sick" (195).

One day while on a shopping trip, she stops into a sex-change office. They offer her a virtual model of what she would look like in a male body. Because she has been an athlete, the modeling looks heavier and heftier than she would like. Not to worry, it's all customizable. But Cleo is not ready to make the change. Instead, they offer her a compromise, a more "androgynous look." And, on the spot, they reduce the size of her breasts. When she arrives home, Jules is less than pleased. She counters, "But I don't ask you when I put on lipstick or cut my hair. It's my body" (200). This argument begins to raise the central question about the relationship between body and person, between body and identity.

He, of course, thinks about his own pleasure, but also about Feather. Cleo can no longer breastfeed. She counters that Jules can breastfeed the baby (another new social norm) or bottle feed her. Jules has never been raised thinking of breastfeeding as one of his duties or options, has never seen his body in that role, has never seen himself fulfilling that function. He says it would feel "silly" (202). He opts for bottle feeding. And because he will be feeding her, he begins to take her to work with him. Cleo reacts negatively, though, because Jules won't take on the mothering/nurturing role "as a female" (210).

The proverbial straw appears the next time Cleo has sex, on her back. Jules has always preferred top position during sex. Cleo has gone along with it, though she, too, would prefer to be on top. This time, she insists, and he resists. For him, he cannot separate it from her interest in changing. He cannot separate it from her questioning of gender and sex roles. For him, it feels like an attempt at reversing the roles, at domination. Frustrated, she leaves.

As the news article had told her, Changers tend to commingle. They prefer one another's company, and they frequent specialized bars. She finds the Oophyte because she's "still curious" (205). (An oophyte is the gametophyte of mosses and ferns; they create gametes via mitosis.) At the bar, the lighted sign has an alternating plus sign and arrow attached to the O. It revolved so that "[o]ne moment the plus sign was inside and the arrow out, the next moment the reverse" (205). While the name of the bar suggests a rupturing of the reproductive imperative of heterosexual futurity, the reality inside the bar doesn't live up to the hype. In the bar, she has sex with Saffron, who has changed sex many times. Saffron tells her that the body into which one is born does not matter, and warns her that changing sexes will not solve any of her problems. Cleo asks Saffron if he had been born female. He responds, "It's no longer important how I was born. I've been both. It's still me on the inside" (207). Saffron suggests then that identity is not bodily but cognitive.

Following her encounter at the Oophyte, Cleo orders the creation of her cloned body. She will have six months to wait until it is fully grown. She informs Jules of her decision; he reminds her that he will not "follow her" in her decision (208). He says that when she walks into the house in a male body, he may not be able to see her in the same way anymore. Cleo responds, "You could if you were a woman" (208). Here, again, we see the heteronormativity that permeates the story.

Six months later, Cleo wakes up in a male body. Cleo and the text then shift to Leo and to masculine pronouns (he/him). While the children—who have grown up with changing as a social commonplace—hardly notice, Jules is not happy. He brings a woman home for revenge sex, but Leo joins them. They also discover that the revenge lover is also a Changer.

Leo returns to the Oophyte, and he is propositioned by several women. When he cannot "perform" (209) for Lynx, they commiserate. Lynx does not want to hurt Leo's "male ego" (214). Lynx suggests to Leo, "Don't be a man. Be a male human, instead" (215). Jules and Leo become buddies. Leo feels more "whole" than ever before and can see that Jules is "not whole" (219). Eventually, though, Leo and Jules do have sex. What, then, were Jules's reservations? Social mores had changed, and the stigma of same-sex sex seemed to have disappeared. Jules's hang-up seemed to be that, for him, Cleo's identity, and his love for her, resided in her body.

Leo returns to a female body, but does not return to being Cleo. That person is gone. She (her pronouns always follow her body choice) is now some holistic combination of Cleo and Leo, and adopts the moniker Nile. She tells Jules, "What you have to understand is that they're both gone, in a sense" (222).

Several things become apparent after reading the story. For one, it operates from a particular binary perspective on identities. For another, it assumes a particular relationship between the body and identity.

On the one hand, I would commend Varley for taking on the issue. Far too much SF has simply assumed traditional gender roles, even in radically altered futures. As Veronica Hollinger writes in "(Re)Reading Queerly," science fiction has traditionally been an "overwhelmingly *straight*" narrative form (24). True, many New Wave and feminist science fiction writers had already addressed gender roles and sex roles by 1979. Still, Varley addresses the issues of body and identity, and body and sexuality squarely and centrally.

Varley may have also been aware of the emergence of Queer Studies in the 1970s. The first undergraduate course on the topic of homosexuality was offered at UC Berkeley in the spring of 1970 (MacNaron, 168), and Varley was living in San Francisco around that time. Regardless, the story, in some ways, parallels the real-life story of Christine Jorgensen, the first known US citizen to undergo gender confirmation surgery (GCS). (I am not suggesting that Varley consciously or unconsciously took Jorgensen as a model, only noting the similarities.) Jorgensen returned from a stint in the Army and attended college and read an article about GCS. Jorgensen then traveled to Denmark for the initial surgeries, and completed them in the United States. Her transition was front-page news in New York in the early 1950s, and she was hailed as having paved the way for trans individuals who followed. In 1951, Jorgensen wrote in a letter to friends:

> As you can see by the enclosed photos, taken just before the operation, I have changed a great deal. But it is the other changes that are so much more important. Remember the shy, miserable person who left America? Well, that person is no more and, as you can see, I'm in marvelous spirits.
> (Jorgensen, 1967, 105)

The sentiments here echo the discussions between Cleo and Saffron. For Jorgensen, she was dissatisfied with her body, and the change in bodies was integral to her sense of self and her self-satisfaction. While the change is not quite as clear-cut for Cleo, Cleo does experience dissatisfaction, and Nile does feel more whole (and arguably more satisfied) after having experienced life (and sex) in female and male bodies—the modern-day Tiresias. Nile tells Jules that both Cleo and Leo are gone, just as Christine says that the person who left the United States is gone.

And yet "Options" seems to miss the mark in a number of other areas. For one, the story assumes a binary identity. Both before and after surgery, Changers seem to have only two options: female bodies or male bodies. True, they can customize the degree of femininity or masculinity and can sculpt the body to fit a personal self-image. Even so, the options remain binary. That binary is reinforced when Cleo wants Jules to "follow" her into changing. Although they both seem to have little hesitation with taking lovers of either sex, Cleo seems to believe that they should both change in order to maintain the heterosexual dyad. She also seems irritated that Jules will excel at "mothering" while in a male body. For Cleo, cis-het remains the normative standard.

The Oophyte sign, while on the one hand a symbol rupturing the sexual reproductive order, at the same time reinforces the binary options of male and female. At Oophyte, Cleo initially has sex with Saffron, who identifies as a man (though has changed many times). Her initial impulse is to maintain the heteronormative relationship, even while in a place situated outside the norms of society. After the change, Leo returns to Oophyte and is propositioned by three women. So, even as Leo pursues a heterosexual relationship, the three women from Oophyte do as well.

The other area that seems to miss the mark is complexity of the relationship between self and body. During Cleo's first trip to Oophyte, Saffron says the body does not matter, that it's the same person inside. During the second trip to the bar, Lynx tells Leo that she does not want to hurt Leo's "male ego." Clearly the social function and value of the body has changed in Varley's future world. Children casually go off to school in the nude. The only shame is of class, not body or sexuality. And yet, Cleo makes it clear that living inside her body, having sex as a woman, giving birth to children, breastfeeding them, playing sports have *all* had an effect on her identity and her sense of self. So, does the body "not matter?" Leo's male ego isn't damaged because Leo has not lived the life with the expectations of masculinity. Cleo makes that clear in her relationship with Jules.

Part of the difficulty that "Options" faces, then, is the way in which it assumes gender and sexuality as an essentialized identity. Of course, it's not fair to judge "Options" according to theoretical understandings of 2021. At the time Varley published "Options," feminist theorists were already rejecting gender as an essential identity in favor of a discursive construct in the 1970s. For example, in 1979—the same year Varley published "Options"—Esther Newton published *Mother Camp*, a study of drag queens in which Newton makes the claim that drag ruptures the connection between sexed body and gendered behavior. Newton's study was groundwork for the full-fledged arguments of Judith Butler's *Gender Trouble* (1990), which argues that gender is a performance of a social norm.

So, "Options" appears at a moment of theoretical and conceptual change. While the story offers a view of sex, gender, and sexuality that might seem outmoded in 2021, it remains an insight into the history of our conceptualizations of sex, gender, and sexuality. It takes identity as an essence. The person exists regardless of, and in spite of, the body. And, yet, the experiences one has in a different body matter, and they do affect the person's wholeness. The characters in "Options" *do* have some options, though they are limited by the operational model of sex, gender, and sexuality as binaries. As long as we're offered a static set of choices (for birth certificates, driver's licenses, passports), we will be limited in our options. What queer theory and performance theory offer is the notion of sex and gender as a set of practices that we engage in, that shape us as we engage in them, but do not adhere as essential elements of the self.

And in that model, we have options.

2. Swastikas Tonight

> *Everything's fantastic if it's out of the lines*
> *you're brought up on.*
> —Burdekin, *Swastika Night*

POST 2016 ELECTION (in the United States), Amazon saw several books skyrocket back to the top of the sales charts, including *1984* and *The Handmaid's Tale*. The former was first published in 1949 and the latter in 1986. The politics of the 2010s made these two books seem politically relevant again. Orwell's *1984* was written in postwar Britain as a warning against Communism. The novel's representation of totalitarian regimes resonates with 21st-century readers living in the midst of a new wave of fascism. Atwood's *Handmaid's Tale* was written in Canada in the midst of the rise of the New Right in the United States. The novel's representation of a patriarchal and theocratic regime similarly resonates with contemporary readers living in the midst of a new wave of misogyny, homophobia, and white nationalism.

Another book that seems relevant again is Katharine Burdekin's (she/her) *Swastika Night* (1937), in ways that intersect with both Orwell and Atwood. Burdekin was a British writer (1896-1963) who wrote a few SF novels, several utopian novels, three of which were published under the pen name, Murray Constantine. *Swastika Night* was originally published as by Constantine.

Originally published by Victor Gollanz in the UK, the novel had slipped into obscurity, though it was revived in 1985 by the Feminist Press, featuring a forward by Daphne Patai (she/her). Gollanz reissued the novel in 2016 in its Gollanz SF Masterworks series. The novel has been examined by (feminist) SF scholars from time to time, most recently by queer theorist Alexis Lothian (she/her) in the monograph, *Old Futures: Speculative Fiction and Queer Possibility* (2018). Lothian considers *Swastika Night* alongside Charlotte Haldane's (she/her) *Man's World* (1926) as examples of between-the-wars dystopias that take up rising concerns about eugenics. Lothian suggests that Haldane's novel is "speculative poison [and] a pure technology of genocide" (67). In the novel, the post-national scientists have created a way to maintain a purely white world via a deadly poison (Thanatil) that targets dark skin pigmentation. Lothian adds that Thanatil "might have been a utopian dream for Nazi scientists and white supremacists alike" (67).

While Haldane seems to buy into the eugenic rhetoric and the separatist politics of fascism, Burdekin seems to be appalled by it. Instead of a celebratory, utopian narrative, Burdekin offers an oppressive, dystopian vision of the future under the Nazis. Mind you, Burdekin was writing this novel in 1935 and '36. Hitler (born 1889) fought in World War I, received two military decorations, and was recovering in the hospital when word of the Armistice came down. Hitler blamed Germany's defeat on insufficiently patriotic Germans. Shortly thereafter, he joined the German Worker's Party, which combined nationalist rhetoric with interest in worker's welfare. By 1920, Hitler had risen through the ranks and had become head of the Party's propaganda wing. The party was renamed the National Socialist German Workers Party (Nazi) and adopted the hakenkreuz (swastika) as its symbol. By 1923, following the Beer Hall Putsch in which the Nazis crashed a meeting by another right-wing leader, Hitler was recognized as a national leader. He was jailed for his role in the Putsch, and, during his time in jail, he formulated what would become *Mein Kampf*.

Published in 1925, the book articulated his nationalistic and anti-Semitic views.

Hitler continued to develop the Nazi party, including the Hitler Youth and the Schutzstaffel (SS), but the global economic depression of 1929 destabilized the Weimar Republic—a situation on which Hitler capitalized. By January 1933, Hitler was named chancellor, a date that marks the beginning of the Third Reich, aka the Thousand-Year Reich. The Reich was intended to fulfill Hitler's dream of a national and racial purity; in order to create the Lebensraum, the Germans would need a leader, der Führer. World War II officially broke out in September 1939 when Germany invaded Poland.

None of this buildup was secret. It was in the news. Presumably, Burdekin was aware of the rise of Adolf Hitler. She heard the rhetoric. She saw the violence. She saw the demonization of the Other. And it terrified her. In an essay entitled, "Myth and Archetype in Science Fiction," Ursula K. Le Guin (she/her) writes that the science fiction writer, the modern myth maker, must look into herself and find what truly frightens her. It's what Mary Shelley (she/her) did, and she created Dr. Frankenstein. It's what Katharine Burdekin did. She extrapolated Hitler's ideology and vision into a nightmarish novel.

The novel posits a world in which the Nazis prevail, and they rule approximately half the world (the Japanese Empire rules the rest). But the Nazis have done their best to erase all of history and to simultaneously create a mythology around the historical figure of Hitler and to replace that with a religion of Hitler. In the novel, the Jews have been completely eliminated, and Christians constitute the marginal Other. Christianity represents an ideology that might threaten Hitlerianism, so it must be destroyed, too. In the year 720 After Hitler, a visitor from England arrives in Germany with the aim of destroying the Nazi empire. Luckily, he finds an ally in the local Knight.

Burdekin notes, too, the misogyny that accompanies the Nazi Party. As Alfred and the Knight discuss the current state of gender and gender relations, they note that women are barely above animals. But Alfred works out the idea that "women are not women." He means to suggest that the "women" who live in captivity in the Women's Quarters are not "women" but are what the men have made them into. Consequently, "women" have never existed since women have *always* lived in a society in which men shape them into their own images and into their own uses. And while he understands this principle in theory, he cannot quite overcome his biases against women in practice.

So, too, with sexuality. Since women are effectively eliminated from German society (though women are forced to have sex for reproductive purposes), the men live entirely within the company of men. While the references are often subtle and sometimes coded, the novel suggests that the men engage in sex with one another. But instead of suggesting that the homosexuality of the German men is the pathological effect of Nazism, or a defect in a same-sex society, Alfred's argument about women points to a social explanation. Just as the women are, the men too are shaped by their surrounding social and political norms. They cannot help but be what society expects and allows. What would the men be like absent the horrors of the Nazi regime? What would Hermann be had the Nazis not shaped him? That very question devastates Hermann.

My students were fully on board with the novel's take on essentialism and constructionism. They saw that Burdekin articulated a nuanced (if sometimes graphic) take on gender and sexuality. They also noted the eerie similarities between Hitler and the Nazis of *Swastika Night* and Donald Trump (he/him) and the Republican party. Even as I tried to steer them to think about the global reemergence of fascism and the words and deeds of other fascist leaders (Rodrigo Duterte, Recep

Tayyip Erdoğan, Vladimir Putin), they made the connections to their own lives, to their own current political reality. And it scared them. They hear the rhetoric; they see the demonization of the racial, ethnic, and sexual Other; they see the deification of Trump.

The question, of, course, is what they do next....

3. Sex and/or Dangerous Visions

> *What you hold in your hands is more than a book. If we are lucky, it is a revolution.*
> —Harlan Ellison, Introduction, *Dangerous Visions*

IT IS A commonplace to say that revolution was in the air in the 1960s. The civil rights movement, the women's liberation movement, the Black Panther Party, La Raza Unida, the sexual revolution, youth counterculture, anti-war activism, and ecological warriors all sought radical and sudden changes in power, in social and political structures and practices. Revolution was in the works for science fiction, too. The New Wave writers and feminist writers sought to redefine the genre, its parameters, and its reach.

"Aye…and Gomorrah" by Samuel R. Delany (he/him) and "Sex and/or Mr. Morrison" by Carol Emshwiller (she/her) both pushed at sex, gender, and sexual boundaries. The two stories originally appeared in Harlan Ellison's (he/him) anthology, *Dangerous Visions* (1967). Agent, author, and provocateur Ellison liked to push buttons and boundaries. He liked to shock, and—even more than that—he didn't like to be told what to write. Ellison's premise was that he would publish an anthology of science fiction that would not, and *could* not, be published anywhere else. He contacted a number of authors and told them that he would impose no limitations. In the end, he published thirty-three pieces by thirty-two writers, some well-known, others not so much.

The results were mixed, and the critics were conflicted, but the SF reading public seemed to be on board. The book itself won a Hugo Award (voted on by reading fans of SF), Philip José Farmer's (he/him) "Riders of the Purple Wage" won a Hugo for Best Novella, and Fritz Leiber's (he/him) "Gonna Roll the Bones" won for Best Novelette. Several other stories were finalists. The readers in 1967, the readers of SF responded positively to these stories designed to challenge expectations and taboos.

"Sex and/or Mr. Morrison" pushes the boundaries of what a science fiction story is, does, and addresses. Doubtless it would not have been published in one of the many SF magazines at the time. Delany's story, too, would have found a hard time. Although his story clearly fits into the science fiction mode, the subject matter would have been a tough sell in 1967.

Emshwiller's story centers upon an unnamed woman. She lives just below Mr. Morrison, her tenant. The thing is, Mr. Morrison is a large man. From the perspective of 2021, the story could be read as fat shaming. For one, I don't think it was Emshwiller's intent. For another, my students didn't think so. Nevertheless, the woman does comment on his size, repeatedly, and it might well trigger a negative response in someone reading it now. The woman's real intent is to find out if he is one of the Others. She has become convinced that more than two sexes exist. One day, as she sat through a matinée performance of Stravinsky's revolutionary work *Rite of Spring*, watching the dancers in their "naked suits," she began to wonder if we are mistaken to assume that there are only two sexes. Surely, Other sexes must exist. But who are they? Where are they? Is Mr. Morrison one of them? She adds, "It is not out of fear or disgust that I am looking for them. I am open and unprejudiced" (332).

She decides to sneak into his apartment and see for herself. She hides in his closet; she sleeps among his dirty clothes;

she nibbles cheese and Fig Newtons beneath his desk. And then he comes home. And he undresses. Though she initially believes that she has seen Mr. Morrison's genitals, they are not of the expected variety. What she ultimately realizes is that it may be another "naked suit." She flees down the stairs into her own home and waits for him to come find her. Surely "he must (mustn't he) come after me for what I saw" (336).

Delany's story centers upon a group of Spacers. These individuals were chosen as children to participate in the Spacer program. They are neutered (gonads and organs removed) and then trained to work in space. Spacers build stations, mine water, and provide resources for Earth. But the radiation in space would have long-term effects on them, and any offspring would be likely to have defects as a result. So, in order to curb population overall, and in order to limit birth defects, they are all neutered. As a result, they never pass through the usual physical maturation process.

At the beginning of the story, a group of Spacers arrive back on Earth for a "shore leave." In Paris, they encounter a group of gay men in a public bathroom. The gay men warn them of the police presence and suggest that "you…people" (534) should leave. They go to Texas, and there they meet the prostitutes waiting for the shrimp fishermen to disembark. One of the prostitutes suggests that the Spacers are distracting the prostitutes' clientele, and that "you…people" (535) should leave.

You see, people have developed a sexual fetish for Spacers. While the technical term is "free-fall-sexual-displacement complex, (540), everyone just calls them *frelks*. The frelks desire the Spacers; they want to have sex with them; they seek them out and pay them. The politics of frelks divides our group of Spacers. Some see it as debauched and degrading, while others see it as a legitimate exploitation and source of money. If people are willing to pay….

In Istanbul, they divide up, and our unnamed protagonist finds a young art student. She wants to go to her room with him (it is the pronoun used in the story), but she cannot pay him. Her room is filled with Spacer porn: posters, magazines, and lurid novels. When he asks that she give him something of value to her, she refuses. She is ashamed of herself, of her "perversion." When he suggests that she change, she yells, "You don't choose your perversions" (511). In the end, he leaves the apartment, neither one able to provide what the other one wanted. Through the early encounter between the spacers and the gay men in the pissoir, to the encounter with the frelk in the apartment, Delany draws the reader's attention to the story's resonances for queer folx in the United States. Delany was an African-American gay man living in New York City at the time. He writes in his autobiography, *The Motion of Light on Water*, about such public encounters with other gay men. When the frelk says that she did not choose her "perversion," her words echo those of many queer folx.

These two stories from 1967 appeared in an anthology designed to challenge norms, and they both queered the genre. On the one hand, Emshwiller makes us look at the genre of SF (science fiction, or speculative fiction) differently. "Sex and/or Mr. Morrison" challenges us to consider what SF is and what it can do. But more than that, the story asks us to think about sex differently. The narrator thinks that we have been wrong all along to define sex as a binary. She says, "I accept. I accept…. I will love, I already love, whatever you are" (318). She is wholly unafraid of the Other; she is eager to accept Otherness into her life.

Similarly, Delany's story invites us to think about sexual "deviance" or "perversion." Whereas Emshwiller's story makes the familiar world strange, Delany's story makes the strange seem familiar. While the frelks are generally demeaned—by society, by most of the Spacers—the narrator and the art student offer more sympathetic representations. Frelks (all too similar to "freaks") are marginalized in society, but they cannot help who they are, or what they are attracted to. The frelks may seem strange or unusual to readers—they are a new concept, after all—but the story makes them familiar. In doing so, Delany asks the reader to queer their perspective, their understanding of sexual identity, their attitudes and responses to "perversion," since perversion is always defined against the dominant practices.

From the perspective of 2021, the stories may seem tame, depending on the reader's experience. But in 1967, they were revolutionary. Read as history, read as part of the archive of SF, they provide insight into the development of the genre and of our thinking about sex, gender, and sexuality. Beyond that, though, these stories still have the ability to queer the genre and to queer one's perspective.

4. Listening to the Female Man

> *Listen to the female man.*
> —Joanna Russ, *The Female Man*

LITERARY THEORY HAS played a central role in feminism and queer theory. Theorists such as Sandra Gilbert (she/her) and Susan Gubar (she/her) developed a model for reading women's writing. Elaine Showalter (she/her) developed a taxonomy that pointed to the ways in which women were redefining writing, were writing from and as women. The queer theorist Eve Kosofsky Sedgwick (she/her) helped develop queer theory through, in part, her models of reading. In science fiction, Joanna Russ (she/her) wrote extensively on the field, on feminist writing, and the ways in which the tropes of science fiction reinforce patriarchy. In much of her writing, she sought to redefine the genre.

Russ was New York City born and bred. She was admitted to—but did not attend—the Bronx High School of Science and was a top-ten selection in the Westinghouse Science Talent Search competition. Nevertheless, she attended Cornell University (English major) and Yale School of Drama (Master of Fine Arts). Russ firmly and consistently identified as a feminist. She later identified as a lesbian. The catalyst for coming out was the "Intercession Program on Women" at Cornell University in January 1969. Both Betty Friedan (she/her) and Kate Millett (she/her) were there, and the event changed Russ forever. After Cornell, she was filled with rage and later said that *The Female Man* came "right out of [her] guts" (Perry, 295).

She was an active participant in the SF community, engaging with both SF writers and SF fans. She steadfastly advocated for changes within SF, in writing, in publishing, and in reading. She steadfastly advocated for more kinds of story lines, more kinds of characters. While much of her nonfiction writing is relegated to the annals of magazines and fandom, she collected and published many of her essays in *How to Suppress Women's Writing* (1983), *Magic Mommas, Trembling Sisters* (1985), *To Write Like a Woman: Essays in Science Fiction and Feminism* (1995), *What Are We Fighting For: Sex, Race, Class and the Future of Feminism* (1998), and *The Country You Have Never Seen: Essays and Reviews* (2007).

The short story, "When It Changed," was published in 1972 in Harlan Ellison's second anthology, *Again, Dangerous Visions*. It garnered the Nebula Award for best Short Story in 1973, was a finalist for the Hugo Award in 1973, and earned a retrospective James Tiptree (now Otherwise) Award in 1995. The story is set on a distant planet, Whileaway. Humans had fled pollution and degradation, looking for a new world. They found one, but the planet struck back. An indigenous bacterium or virus wiped out all the men, leaving the planet populated solely by women for 600 years. The trope of a single-sexed society is hardly new. Hundreds of them have been written over the past century. Russ, however, makes a few changes to the trope.

A new ship arrives; humans of Earth had not learned their lesson. They now seek "fresh," untainted human DNA. But the all-male crew that disembarks sees paradise in front of them—an all-female world—and they decide to stay. The residents of Whileaway object. While Janet argues with them over the definitions of "unnatural" and "human," her wife Katy picks up a gun to shoot them all. Janet stops her. I would argue that this scene is generally misread. Readers and critics alike have read it as pessimistic, as the inevitable collapse and failure of all-female societies. The original name of the colony had been "For a While," suggesting that they would not remain on the planet. Critics often suggest that the good times must come to an end with the return of men to their society. They were a single-sex society only for a while, and now men will return.

I would suggest that the scene represents something both more positive and more diabolical. Janet stops Katy's act of violence for three reasons. (1) Janet is a Peace Officer and is bound to follow the law. (2) Janet knows that Katy hates guns and violence. Therefore, Janet—who *has* killed people—spares her wife the trauma. (3) Janet remembers what killed the men in the first place—the planet. The men can only return "for a while," and the planet will wipe them out again. They can accomplish their goals without bloodying their own hands.

But in full second-wave feminism mode, the story challenges 1972 notions of sex and gender roles, and the relationship between the two (remember, Gayle Rubin [she/her] articulated the sex/gender system in 1975). The characters develop a wide range of human capabilities and preferences, regardless of their sexed bodies. Residents of Whileaway are fully human; residents of Earth are only ever half human. The story also queers notions of the family. While the women initially repopulate the planet via parthenogenesis, they develop the technical means to merge ova. The latter technique offers at least two advantages: (1) it minimizes inherited genetic anomalies, and (2) it creates two biological parents who are invested in the child. The child—the daughter—carries the patronymic of the person who carried her to term.

While presented as a utopian alternative to sex and gender on our own world, Whileaway also has a darker side. The girls and women are free to be themselves, but they are also constrained by Whileawayan norms and practices. All Whileawayans are taken out into the woods and left to fend for themselves. Some make it; some do not. The practice is harsh but designed to strengthen the individual and the society. They are also kept to fairly strict timelines. For example, at 30 they are given five years to reproduce—a practice that seems to compel reproduction of everyone.

Given the success of "When It Changed," Russ was encouraged to expand the story into a novel. She did, and it was published in 1975, though the path to publication was far from easy. Many publishers rejected it outright; others said that they had already done a feminist novel, so, no thanks. After the novel was finally published, some critics praised the novel (R. D. Mullen [he/him] and Donna Perry [she/her], for example); others were harsh in their assessment. Richard Harter (he/him) calls her a "crank"; Michael Goodwin (he/him) calls the novel "a scream of anger" (qtd. in Russ, "Recent"); Lester Del Rey (he/him) calls it a "truly schizophrenic novel"; Alexei (he/him) and Cory Panshin (she/her) call it "self-indulgent" and "solipsistic." And, yet, I would argue it's a masterpiece. Those critics fail to understand the intent; they fail to understand the goals; and they fail to understand the ways in which *The Female Man* queers SF, gender, the family, the protagonist, and the form of the novel itself. Those critics read the novel according a set of conventions and expectations that Russ had rejected.

Reading *The Female Man* is no walk in the park. While Russ challenges sexual and gender roles in "When It Changed," she challenges *everything* in her novel. It takes place in four separate time continua, each occupied by an individual who shares the same genotype. The four Js are Janet, Joanna, Jeannine, and Jael. Though genotypically identical, they differ in appearance and in circumstance. Joanna occupies a "world zero," a reality that looks very similar to Joanna Russ's own world in the early 1970s when she was writing the book. But do not assume that "Joanna" the character is a stand-in for Joanna the writer. Janet resides in Whileaway, which is quite similar to the Whileaway from the story. She arrives in Joanna's world and offers a comparison with our own world. Jeannine lives in New York, but it is a New York in which the great depression never ended. Her circumstances and options are bleak. Jael comes from Womanland, a single-sex society that is literally at war with Manland, the metaphorical Battle of the Sexes of the '60s and '70s made manifest.

Janet is a lesbian and seems appalled by, well, everything in Joanna's world—*our* world. She cannot read the gender codes and the sexual norms, and so she shocks everyone. Jael is also lesbian, though she also has sex with her male house-robot, Davy. Jeannine is cis-het, but not at all happy with her boyfriend. However, she has read all the fairy tales and romance novels, and she knows how it's *supposed* to go. That's what she wants. And Joanna? She's questioning everything. Her identity, her sexuality, her gender, her profession, and her manners. She discovers anger. In a scene late in the book, she slams a man's fingers in a car door. Not accidentally. Not for something he had done. Out of anger. Anger at the whole damned system.

Let's not forget Laura Rose. She is a teenager in Joanna's world, a young woman who is also angry at the world and her assigned lot in it. Janet takes her under her wing and helps her work through questions of her identity and her sexuality.

Russ, as I noted above, queers SF conventions. Sure, we have multiple time continua and futuristic sex robots, but the novel is really about us, about our social norms. She queers the notion of a protagonist, of a literary character. For one, they are all women and half of them are lesbians. But even more, the reader can never be certain of the narrative "I." Who is speaking? Which of the four Js? She queers the notion of a unified self. Readers tend to want to read the four Js as aspects of one person, but they are not. They do not make up the various aspects of Joanna. Readers tend to want some resolution of the characters in the end, which Russ refuses. And she queers what a novel does. Russ has argued that the very form of the novel is built around the individual (though we can see exceptions such as Toni Morrison's [she/her] *The Bluest Eye* and Sandra Cisneros's [she/her] *The House on Mango Street*), and *The Female Man* is not about that.

The novel certainly has its limitations and shortcomings. For one, the articulation of both sex and gender are largely binary. Joanna writes of becoming a woman (à la Simone de Beauvoir [she/her]) and then becoming the female man of the title. As the four Js struggle with their assigned gender roles, they seem to see themselves as limited to two options. Joanna says she *is* a man; Jeannine says she wouldn't be a man for *anything*. Jael resides in Womanland, which is at war with Manland, and the two territories are the only options. However, the residents of Whileaway simply do not understand binary gender. They are each different, and they are each fully human. Masculine pronouns have not existed in their language for nearly 600 years.

Even so, in Womanland, Jael introduces the other Js to the Changed. Because the men in Manland have no women, the women of Womanland send over batches of male babies, who are then socialized to be "real men." But for some of them, the indoctrination does not take, and they are then surgically converted to women, called the Changed. A small portion of those do not become women but inhabit a space in between called Half-Changed. The process does suggest that the relationship between sex and gender is neither fixed nor essential. Many of the male babies fail (in Manland's terms) to successfully socialize into "real men," perhaps due to genetics, perhaps due to environment, but probably some combination of the two.

On the one hand, Manland is the one place in the novel that is not rigidly binary. An option in between exists. On the other hand, the representations of the Changed are not particularly flattering. They are wildly exaggerated simulations of femininity. The Changed, though, are caught in this

Battle of the Sexes. They must fulfill the men's expectations of femininity, and they are warped by the women's desire for revenge on the men. In this way, the scene can be read as anti-trans. The process in Manland does not allow agency for the Changed—they are failed men who are compelled into a secondary and subservient role. The scenes in Manland, then, seem to suggest that trans women are failed men—a notion thoroughly rejected today. Instead, the scene could also be read as something specific to the horrors of Jael's time continuum. The Changed can also be read as a symptom of the ways in which the gender war limits and shapes all of us. Cheryl Morgan (she/her), a queer SF writer, writes in a blog post on the origins of transphobia: "There's a passage in Joanna Russ's *The Female Man* where the heroines express surprise that trans women learn how to beautify themselves, despite being raised by men. I guess Russ was thinking about the issues, even then" (blog, 2011). Morgan also notes in a memorial blog post that Russ, unlike some of her contemporaries, engaged with trans women as a way to understand and represent them. As no one in Womanland or Manland comes off particularly well, the novel suggests that we are all shaped—and harmed—by the discourses that surround us. All the Js—Joanna, Jeannine, Janet, and Jael—demonstrate that. Even so, that harm is not distributed equally.

Because Russ rejects and redefines so many of the elements of reading (character identification, chronology, unity, resolution, narrative conventions), it leaves readers feeling, well, queer. And that, I would argue, is the whole point....

5. A Body of Excess

I belong in this twilight that hatched me. Or do I?
—Tanith Lee, *Don't Bite the Sun*

FOR CENTURIES FEMINISTS have been caught between two competing philosophical arguments: the body is irrelevant versus the body is constitutive of identity. Some feminists followed the lead of René Descartes (he/him) who argued that the body was irrelevant. For him and his followers, human subjectivity existed as a disembodied, thinking mind. For others, though, being in a body had all kinds of consequences, from what we can sense, to what we can know, and an embodied experience always affects those things. As we saw in Shade 1, John Varley had offered a take on embodiment. The British speculative writer Tanith Lee (she/her) does, as well.

Lee was primarily known as a writer of high fantasy and horror. Indeed, she won a number of fantasy and horror awards for her work. But occasionally, she veered over into SF territory. Lee was also known as a queer writer, though Lee herself was cis-het, and the ways in which, and the degree to which, she dealt with queer issues developed later in her career.

Lee's first novel was a YA tale called *The Dragon Hoard* (1971). Her second novel was a lengthy high fantasy affair called *The Birthgrave* (1975). That novel set the tone for much her writing to follow. But her third novel was *Don't Bite the Sun* (1976), the first SF one and markedly different from the first two. Her other SF novels include *Drinking Sapphire Wine* (1977, a sequel to *Don't Bite the Sun, Electric Forest* (1979), *The Silver Metal Lover* (1981), and *Metallic Love* (2005, a sequel to

SML). In the end, she published some 90 novels and 300 short stories before her untimely death due to breast cancer.

At the time of her death, Lee was generally beloved in the queer community, as she consistently and persistently wrote about issues of sex, gender, and sexuality. For example, queer writer Lee Mandelo notes that Lee's works were frequently "rather directly queer and feminist" in the ways they appropriated and revised fairy tales and fantasy. Over at *Lambda Literary*, Craig Gidney (he/him) writes that Lee "featured gay, lesbian, bisexual and transgender characters throughout all of her fiction" (2010). KC Redding-Gonzalez (pronouns unknown) writes that Lee "never shied away from LGBT characters, storylines, or situations" (Zombie Salmon, 2019).

So, much of her later work was, perhaps, more overtly focused on queer issues, or, on queering genre expectations of horror and fantasy. And her first SF novel certainly raises and addresses questions of sex and gender, questions of gender and embodiment, and questions of sexuality. But here in this early novel, *Don't Bite the Sun*, Lee seems to shy away from making bolder claims. In the end, I would suggest that the novel reads as profoundly modernist in its foundations and aims, and somewhat conservative in its representations of gender and sexuality.

Don't Bite the Sun extrapolates several social and technological notions to rather absurd dimensions. The novel considers the consequences of rampant consumerism. It also considers the social and environmental effects of longevity technologies. How would society and the world change if each of us lived for hundreds of years? The novel suggests we'd destroy the planet, we'd radically limit reproduction, and we'd enjoy extended childhoods. But more specifically to our purposes, the novel examines the intersection of sex, gender, and embodiment with the easy shift from body to body.

The events of this 1976 novel focus on a young, unnamed narrator. In the fictive world of *Don't Bite the Sun*, humanity is confined to three domed cities: Four BAA, Four BEE, and Four BOO. The natural world has been largely destroyed, but inside the cities are technological Xanadus. Humans have extended the human lifespan; consequently, a new social order restricting reproduction keeps population growth in check. Furthermore, the young and the old exist in largely separate realms. The period of adolescence has been extended to approximately fifty years. All individuals under fifty occupy the category of "Jang," and they are expected to live life to excess, to engage in healthy doses of sex, drugs, and consumption.

For one, *Don't Bite the Sun* literalizes the capitalist economy. Whereas we often say that business is what makes things run, that money is what makes the world go around, etc., here, the consumption of goods and services is channeled into the power plants and makes the three cities run. While, on the one hand, we see the narrative of technological progress in that the city occupants no longer utilize natural resources for energy, we also see that the need for boundless energy has not diminished. The very high-tech world of Four BEE requires a great deal of energy. On the other hand, we can also see that the city inhabitants are consummate consumers. Here in the early 20th-century United States, we are often told that we have a civic duty to purchase things, and, indeed, post 9/11, we were even told that it was a patriotic duty to go out and buy things. We were told that our consumption was necessary to stabilize the economy in the wake of the instability following the attacks on the World Trade Center. We needed to buy goods and services to keep things running. In Four BEE, the city literally cannot run without the inhabitants consuming and paying. They "pay" for their houses, their transportation, their drugs, their entertainment, their pleasures, their marriages and divorces, and their new bodies.

One of the effects of increased longevity and material excess is rampant suicide. The novel begins, "My friend Hergal killed himself again" (9). It is his fortieth suicide. Death, however, is not death but only rebirth. They simply kill themselves and resurrect themselves in a new, pre-ordered body, built to spec. As Lee describes it, the "Limbo robots immediately home in on any suicide or death, and take the 'victim' to Limbo, where they rescue the life spark and replace it in flesh" (300). Regardless of the sex of the deceased, the new body can be either female or male—though they are largely limited to those two options. Further, the vast majority of the main characters tend to desire and inhabit bodies that fall well within (Four BEE) cultural standards of beauty. For example, the narrator kills herself (9th time), and her new body is "pale and slim, with knee-length silver hair and antennae" (10). After the 10th death, her body is "lithe and glamorous" with an "exotic bust and long scarlet hair" (12). Despite the exoticness of scarlet or silver hair and the occasional antenna, the form of the body fits within contemporary hegemonic standards of beauty.

After her failed attempt to have a child, the narrator is depressed. Consequently, she chooses a "terribly ordinary sort of female body. It was thin and fragile, with insignificant breasts and lank straggly hair. I designed it with slow, meticulous, perverted care. I made it too long in the leg and waist, with dark, unvibrant eyes, behind which I could hide and be safe. I was being a weirdo, not as bad as Hatta in the compulsive horror visitation, but strange and alien nevertheless, in a world where almost everyone is beautiful" (94). Within the cultural economy of *Don't Bite the Sun*, only a horribly depressed person could want an "ordinary" or "unvibrant" body. Predictably, though, her depression wears off, and she reverts to her former, beautiful self.

Most of the rest of the narrator's circle of friends also conform to similar standards of beauty and appearance. For example, Hergal gets a new body following a suicide, and according to the narrator, "Her hair was long and twilight mauve, plaited and full of jewelry. She had emeralds pasted on the nipples of her small, delectable breasts, and a groin shield of flowers" (67). She has two friends, however, who do not conform. While Thinta wants to have a cat's body, she must make do with a human body with fur (32). But even Thinta eventually comes 'round. Thinta, who is generally in a male body, gets a new female body, in which, according to the narrator, "She looked very attractive, minus her fur now, with clouds of long green hair and a delicate, chiselled-looking pale body, so unlike her rather hysterically stolid personality" (91).

Hatta, however, almost never conforms to conventional standards. In his first appearance in the novel, he is "fat *and* spotty [...] with three green eyes" (13). Later, Hatta is "huge, bluish, shiny, limpy" with "two heads" (35). The narrator refuses his offer of marriage, saying, "get yourself a reasonable body" (35). Like Mary Shelley's Monster and James Tiptree's Philadelphia Burke, Hatta desires to be loved for who he is rather than what he looks like, though he is rejected by the narrator, and by everyone else. Although, to a certain extent, the reader identifies with Hatta, and to a certain extent we believe that the narrator is unjust in her attitude regarding Hatta and her repeated rejection of him, he represents the marginalization of those who do not conform.

Although the residents of Four BEE have (almost) unlimited possibilities before them in terms of the bodies they construct and inhabit, they return, again and again, to the cultural forms of normativity. When they do deviate from the norm, it is a direct consequence of depression or some other anomaly, or, as in Hatta's case, they are offered to readers as a normative reminder of the consequences of difference. While postmodern critics such as Susan Bordo (she/her) suggest that rampant consumerism contributes to the postmodern subject and suggest that the postmodern subject engages in endless play and subversion (1991), the characters in *Don't Bite the Sun* seem much more concerned with the modernist search for meaning, for transcendence, and for love. At the level of plot, the narrator *does* dissent and question (some) cultural practices and whether she even belongs in Four BEE society. The narrator searches for something more. The boundless consumerism does not fulfill her, and she looks for meaning in adulthood, in work, in art, and in a child.

The fictional construct of the society in *Don't Bite the Sun* also offers the possibility of a postmodern undecidability with regard to gender and sexuality. Fundamentally, however, they are engaged in a deeper search for meaning and identity, one that is predicated on conventional conceptions of gender and sexuality. Although the narrator is "predominantly" female, she does occasionally take on a male body. Upon these occasions, the narrative essentializes the relationship between sex and gender. When the narrator is female, she consistently exhibits feminine characteristics. For example, when the narrator petitions the Committee to have her Status changed from Jang to Adult, she undergoes a series of tests regarding her attitudes, behaviors, tastes, preferences, and so on. Expectedly, she tests "normal" for her age and status, including that she has her "male tendencies nicely coordinated with the female ones" (43). Nevertheless, she exhibits a maternal desire (which is triggered, in part, by her nurturing of the "pet" she steals) and goes in search of males to sire her child. Furthermore, when she does take on a male body, (s)he has a dream wherein (s)he has a small child, for whom (s)he feels "protective and strong" (91). However, instead of watching the combining of the egg and the sperm of her/his potential child, the now-male narrator says, "I felt too emotional and my male impulse was to repress that, so I fled into the night" (91).

Many critics and theorists who have written about gender suggest that gender is not a stable or static category. What one society might call masculine and feminine changes over time, as a result of a complex matrix of political, religious, economic, and technological changes. Therefore, if a society were to develop the ability to shift an individual's identity from one sexed body to a differently sexed body, we might expect to see shifts in the definition and manifestation of gendered attributes. And, indeed, at times it is difficult to read the gender of the secondary characters. Nevertheless, some of the secondary characters still inhabit a space fully within familiar, contemporary definitions. In addition, the fact that the narrator herself replicates, in some ways, conventional gender norms would seem to validate them.

In addition to the replication of essentialized gender norms, the text also rests upon a heteronormative foundation. With individuals swapping sexed bodies at will, the potential for examining the fluidity and multiplicity of sexuality beckons. Nevertheless, *Don't Bite the Sun* seems to favor the heterosexual relationship. For example, the narrator's friend Danor (female) shows up with a dozen or so male, and one or two female, followers, all of whom have a bet to see who she'll have sex with first. The narrator suggests that Danor suicide and come back as male. She responds that she already has, but that the flock all suicided and came back as female. "And she kissed me so sweetly I made an abrupt mental note that, next time I was male and Danor female, it might be an idea to try the floaters again and see if we could do any better that way" (101). This scene suggests that the sexual desire is for a differently sexed body, and not the personality of the individual, which seems remarkably unchanged despite shuttling between differently sexed bodies.

As for the narrator herself, whenever she inhabits a female body, she consistently desires and engages in sex with males.

However, when the narrator takes on a male body, he desires and marries a female, Thinta. Despite the fact that the narrator's desire has always been for males, he now experiences erotic desire for a female simply because his identity now resides in a male body. In effect, in the examples of Danor and her followers, Glar Assule and his team, and the narrator and her/his various lovers, Lee shifts the location of sexuality from the mind to the body.

As Jeffrey Weeks (he/him) summarizes in his book, *Sexuality* (1986), one of the two rival theories on the nature and function of human sexuality is the "essentialist approach" that views "sex as a beneficent force which is repressed by a corrupt civilization" (24). Other essentialists see all cultural practices as manifestations of "basic genetic material." For them, nature provides the "raw material we must use for the understanding of the social" (24). For Weeks and others who take a constructionist approach, then, the basis of sexuality and sexual desire does not rest in the body, but rather in "social forces." Nevertheless, Weeks emphasizes that biology plays a role: "The physiology and morphology of the body provides the preconditions for human sexuality. Biology conditions and limits what is possible. But it does not cause the patterns of sexual life" (25). Furthermore, Weeks argues that the essentialist approach "insists on the fixity of our sexualities" while the constructionist approach allows for a "high degree of fluidity and flexibility in 'human nature,' in its potentiality for change" (54). For Weeks, our sexualities "are not eternally fixed, biologically determined, and unchangeable" (55). Just as Bordo points out that we once conceptualized the body as fixed and later as much more fluid, Weeks suggests that we now consider sexuality as more fluid and malleable.

This would seem to suggest, then, that sexuality resides in the mind and is the product of a complex matrix of personal and cultural histories. Although the body plays some role in defining the possibilities and limits of sexual practices, it does not directly shape sexual desire nor determine the object(s) of sexual desire. In one conversation between the narrator and Hatta, Hatta says, "Can't you see…the body I'm in doesn't matter that much? I'm still me." The narrator insists she would love to have sex with Hatta in a beautiful body.

> "No, no," wailed Hatta.…"I want you—I want *you*. You've been a hundred different bodies; I've wanted you as you are now, as you were with all that silver hair and the antennae, as you were all those [weeks] ago with soft-blue tinted skin and golden eyes. I've wanted you as a male. I've wanted you as you were last, pale and thin, a little nothing girl. Can't you do the same? It's not the body that matters; the physical side is a joke in Four BEE and BAA and BOO. It's irrelevant. It's like wanting someone because they're wearing red toe-rings. Oh, [darling], can't you understand?"
>
> And I almost did. I really almost did. But I couldn't stand the thought of having love with him as he was now. (*DBtS*, 97)

While psychologists and sociobiologists may not routinely imagine what might happen to sexuality if one's personality and identity were switched into a differently sexed body, science fiction writers do. Lee speculates about the ability to freely swap bodies, but in *Don't Bite the Sun* such capabilities would not alter basic gender norms or the hetero-centric assumptions of Western consumer culture. While the characters' sexualities change in *Don't Bite the Sun*, they do not change in the ways that Bordo and Weeks suggest. Whereas Weeks grants the body *some* role in shaping sexuality, Lee grants it the overriding power—at least in the narrator, if not in Hatta. In *Don't Bite the Sun*, the narrator's sexuality is shaped almost

43

entirely by the body she/he inhabits, as the essentialist understanding of sexuality suggests. Inasmuch as an individual character's sexuality changes depending upon the body s/he inhabits, it remains fixed as heterosexual.

6. Queer Families and Queer Gender

The trouble is that we humans, strange beasts that we are, use the same language for taxonomy and identity. By describing ourselves we shape ourselves. All too easily, we become slaves to our self-definitions, so that we cannot tell when they have ceased to be true.
—Raphael Carter, "Not This, Not That"

I SUSPECT EVERYONE has a story like this one: A few years back I was living in an apartment complex. Across the courtyard lived a family with a young daughter, probably four years old. She loved to come across the courtyard to talk to me, to see my dogs, and, especially, to get the mail I would give to her—ads, flyers, and general junk mail. We would chat about the ads. One time, just before Halloween, the flyer featured many ads for costumes. She had strong ideas about costumes and who could wear them. Her ideas about gender, gendered clothing, and gendered roles were already quite firmly set. Girls just cannot wear a firefighter outfit. Girls just cannot be a boy.

In order to look at some early(ish) stories that actively challenge gender assumptions, I'd like to look at four examples. They include "The Third Sex" by Alan Brennert (he/him) (1989), "Congenital Agenesis of Gender Ideation by K. N. Sirsi and Sandra Botkin" by Raphael Carter (zie/zir), "La Cenerentola" by Gwyneth Jones (she/her), and "Lovestory" by James Patrick Kelly (he/him) (all three from 1998). Carter's story won the Otherwise (Tiptree) Award in 1998, and both

Jones's and Kelly's stories were nominated for the Otherwise (Tiptree). (Brennert's pre-dates the Award.)

Brennert's story originally appeared in *Pulphouse* magazine. The story centers around a narrator, Pat, who does not have genitals or gonads. They were born that way. Before they are very old, they already notice that they are different. And when they accidentally see mom and dad having sex, well, that raises all kinds of questions. As one might imagine, childhood is difficult—gym class, sleepovers, swimming in the woods. After they are rejected by a possible lover, they throw themselves wholly into being a girl. But their parents had always dreamed of having a "normal" daughter. After their parents take them to see a specialist who offers to perform what would essentially be a sex-reassignment surgery, they run away.

Once they are away from their hometown, they have the freedom of no prior expectations. They realize that, as much as by their own appearance, gender is produced in the people they meet. Those people bring their own set of expectations, and they frequently just play along with them. But the number of people born without genitals is on the rise. Pat meets others like themselves, but they do not live up to the expectation. They had thought that, perhaps, finding someone just like them would make sense, or maybe even complete them. They eventually find their place with a heterosexual couple. While Pat once believed that they were an atavistic throwback, they now believe that they are an evolutionary step forward.

Gwyneth Jones has an impressive bibliography, with a wide range of work, and awards from a range of genres. "La Cenerentola," which won the British Science Fiction Association's award for best short story, offers a contemporary retelling of the Cinderella fairy tale—but with a few twists. An American couple travels through Europe, with their daughter in tow as they look for the ideal place for a summer home. Their daughter Bobbi had been produced by merging two ova (shades of

Joanna Russ's Whileaway). Along the way, they encounter the Brown family, with two stunningly beautiful daughters, who are clones of their mother. Laura Brown also has a third daughter, Marianina, the plain-looking offspring from a different biological father.

Jones, however, disrupts the reader's expectations. Because the reader knows that the ugly stepdaughter is called Cenerentola (Cinderella), the reader expects certain plot points. For one, the American couple is a lesbian couple, a rare enough sight in a fairy tale. In another disruption, Cinderella's family is beautiful, wealthy, and worldly. The two beautiful daughters are, in the end, the unwanted children. Laura Brown actually favors Marianina. Furthermore, Jones places Laura Brown in the role of Prince Charming. Laura Brown rejects the two refined daughters in favor of the very "authentic" Marianina. The narrator says, "I could feel her troubling allure myself, and I'm no paedophile" (13). Mother is always the first and truest lover.

Raphael Carter, unlike Jones, has a very limited fictional output—one short story and one novel. "Congenital Agenesis of Gender Ideation by N. K. Sirsi and Sandra Botkin" takes the form of an academic paper, which sets out to explore questions of linguistics, and in particular certain forms of cognitive malfunctions. They vacillate between two theories of cognition. When one researcher sets out to determine whether a genetic defect might account for an inability to "apply basic grammatical rules," they instead discover a group of people who cannot see or identify gender. Like those who cannot recognize faces or people (prosopagnosia), these individuals cannot apprehend or distinguish gender (genagnosia). They later discover a set of twins who have a wide range of terms in their own private language that identify and name a wider range of possibilities than do male/female, or man/woman. For example, they would not identify a transgender woman as woman, but rather by their own term, female pseudohermaphrodite. In all, they identified 22 separate categories of identity. In short, the twins "are saying, 'suppose the sexes are like species'" (29).

James Patrick Kelly has a substantial body of genre work almost entirely short fiction. "Lovestory" features the members of a family, on an unknown future alien planet. Aliens have arrived on the planet—whom they call humans. On this planet, a family consists of a mother, a father, and a mam. The mother gestates offspring but then transfers the baby to the mam's pouch when the "scrap" is only a few inches long. For the first few years, the scrap is cared for and raised by the mam. When the scrap leaves, it is given a name by the mother. In this particular family, the mother has decided to leave the family to go study with the aliens (humans). This decision upsets the entire balance of the family. The mother eventually returns to the family in order to give birth and transfer a scrap that had already begun. She is quite clear, though, that she will remain only until the new scrap has left the family and been given a name. Then, she will return to the humans and continue her studies.

In these four stories, two primary issues emerge: the queering of family and the queering of gender.

1. Queering Family

In "The Third Sex," Pat flees a heteronormative, nuclear family because they do not fit. They find no comfort there; further, they find that their parents persist in imposing a normative gender on Pat. In the end, Pat forms a non-normative family with Davy and Lyn, who are a cisgendered couple. But, for one, they have a tendency to argue, and for another, they have been unable to have children. Pat then becomes the third component of the family, a mediator between the two, a balancing third leg. Although they had failed to have children before, once Pat enters the family, they conceive. The new queer familiar arrangement works for Pat and Davy and Lyn.

In "La Cenerentola," Jones queers the family in at least two ways. For one, the narrator's family consists of Thea and Suze and their daughter Bobbi. Same-sex couples are rare enough in fairy tales, but here they have reproduced via the technology of merging ova. They are both biologically Bobbi's parent. The Brown family's two cloned daughters, Celine and Carmen, (like Bobbi) had no father. Both families queer the heteronormative nuclear family, in this case via technology.

Finally, in "Lovestory," Kelly introduces a family that consists of a mother, a father, and a mam. While we know very little about the characters or the structure of their society, it seems to be a normative arrangement. The mother and father produce the child, while the mam rears the child. Although that seems similar to an arrangement where a family might hire a nanny or a wet-nurse, here the mam seems to be a more integral part of the family. The mother had long had her doubts about the family, but when she flees the family to study with the aliens (humans), she learns just how arbitrary their familial arrangement is. Even worse, she finds that it is based on outright lies, suggesting that families are in no way natural and are always social constructs. Although she has learned this, the other members of her family remain heavily invested in the status quo.

2. Queering (Non-Binary) Gender

In "The Third Sex," the narrator Pat refuses to accept themselves as male or female, and they refuse to accept man or woman as defining characteristics. Although their parents push, although their classmates model it, and although everyone Pat meets reads and imposes gender on them, they continue to search until they find a place in which they can be non-binary. At various moments in time, Pat tries to conform to gender norms, but never feels comfortable in them. In addition, Pat thinks that meeting someone else like them, someone else with the very same genetic "anomaly," would feel comfortable. But when they meet Alex, they both decide that it feels too "narcissistic." Further, the story suggests that this is no mere genetic aberration but rather an evolutionary alteration. The third sex (though it never gets named here) will continue to increase in numbers and to become normative.

In "La Cenerentola," Jones plays with the reader's expectations regarding gender. She undermines the gender roles traditionally assigned in fairy tales. In rewriting Cinderella, Jones adds a queer family, eliminates males generally, and Prince Charming particularly. Males are no longer necessary for reproduction; they are not necessary for "rescuing" damsels or unwanted step-daughters. Instead, women provide all of these things for one another. If fairy tales represent and replicate cultural values, then Cinderella promises girls and women that if they are passive, domestic, and (authentically) feminine, they will reap their just rewards. In this retelling of Cenerentola, Marianina embodies none of those traits. Indeed, the locals find her unnerving and see her as a sexual predator, primarily because of the ways in which she steps outside traditional gendered norms.

Finally, in "Congenital Agenesis of Gender Ideation by N. K. Sirsi and Sandra Botkin," Carter multiplies gender and gender categories even more. While the story begins by examining theories of the mind and cognition, it ends with two twins from Minnesota who do not recognize nor categorize gender and sexuality in traditional ways. When they cannot assign a doctor at the hospital with a gender, researchers discover that the doctor is a female pseudohermaphrodite. Because of this difference, the twins cannot identify her as male or female. Instead, they use a term from their own private language. Researchers then learn that the twins have twenty-two categories into which they assign individuals, including "true hermaphrodism, gonadal genesis, and male and female pseudohermaphrodites. They can also categorize individuals with CAID (complete androgen insensitivity disorder). While they initially identify one of the researchers as a woman, they later shift their designation after she had been diagnosed as entering "early menopause." In other words, the twins do not conform to simple binary options. Like the strangers in "The Third Sex" who read social gender cues and then respond to Pat, the twins draw from a completely different set of cues. They had identified and made relevant a different set of characteristics. We each learn to read physical and behavioral cues; we learn which things are "relevant" and which things are "irrelevant." The twins reject those social (and generally binary) norms. For them, sex and gender are large categories containing many possible variations. Instead, they recognize different ways to organize people within those umbrella categories.

Unlike my young neighbor, these four stories, to one degree or another, ask the reader to rethink their gendered assumptions. Queer theory (as an analytical framework) and science fiction (as a mode of reading), fundamentally ask the reader to look at things from a position slightly askew, and these four stories provide a queered perspective on both family and gender.

7. Queering Sex, Love, and SF

By our strangeness we write our bodies into the future.
—Larissa Lai, *Salt Fish Girl*

WHAT DOES THE word "myth" mean to you? Although the word that "myth" derives from means "story," for much of the Western world in the 21st century, "myth" means made-up tale to explain the natural world. God/the gods brought order to chaos; a chariot pulls the sun across the sky; a nymph in the woods calls out the last words of someone's voice. In the 21st century in the West, those tales are seen as outmoded, as insufficient, as silly. They are no longer "active" beliefs, and they have been replaced by scientific explanations. The Big Bang brought about the origins of the universe; the Earth rotates, and the sun appears to move across the sky; sound waves bounce off of solid material and return to the speaker. But are these two sets of stories mutually exclusive? Incompatible?

Larissa Lai (she/her) was born in La Jolla, California, grew up in Canada, and holds Canadian citizenship. Lai's career has taken an interesting path, with a mixture of creative writing, critical writing, and activism, primarily around issues of immigration and immigrants within Canada. She is the author of three novels, including *When Fox Is a Thousand* (1995), *Salt Fish Girl* (2002), and *Tiger Flu* (2018).

If we look at her entire body of work, Lai would seem to be concerned with questions of subjectivity, nationality, and identity. In all of her work, Lai is concerned with conditions of being, definitions of self, and the ability to define oneself. She is also concerned with the world, how it is constructed, and who fits in it. Just who gets to call themselves Canadian, and just who sets or defines the limits? In addition, she considers the intersection of East and West, of Chinese and Canadian cultures, values, and practices. Her fiction offers a view from an askew perspective; it makes readers reconsider their easy presuppositions about the world in which they live.

Salt Fish Girl has received a fair bit of critical attention. To date, critics of *Salt Fish Girl* have examined questions of literary genre (fairy tale, mythology, science fiction), literary and cultural allusions (*The Tempest, Frankenstein, The Little Mermaid, Blade Runner*), border fictions, border control, immigration in Canada, racialized labor exploitation in Canada, transfeminism, Asians-as-aliens, and cyborgs. However, for the purposes of this book, I suggest that *Salt Fish Girl* queers a variety of things, including the nature of sex and desire, reproduction, mythology, and Western science. In the end, *Salt Fish Girl* illustrates an intersection of Chinese mythology and science fiction, culminating in the offspring of those two merged.

The novel's chapters alternately focus on the two protagonists, Nu Wa and Miranda. The five chapters dedicated to Nu Wa begin at some point prior to 1766 BCE. In chapter one, Nu Wa, a snake goddess and a creative deity in Chinese mythology, tells of the creation of the world and of the creation of humans. The novel beings with the familiar line, "In the beginning," but from that point on, Lai repeatedly confounds the tradition of the creation story. In Lai's version, woman does not derive from man but, rather, directly from the female deity. Eventually, Nu Wa falls in love with the Salt Fish Girl (the daughter of a fish salesman), and they run away together, only to live in abject poverty. Distraught, Nu Wa leaves China and the Salt Fish Girl for the Island of Mist and Forgetfulness, only to be duped, incarcerated, and exploited. Eventually, she "made herself as small as a worm, crawled through the tiny aperture of the barely opened bud, and coiled [herself] round and round its small black heart" (208). She hides, like a snake, in the durian fruit and waits for someone to eat the fruit.

The five alternating chapters dedicated to Miranda Ching are set in the near-future enclave Serendipity (near Vancouver) between 2044 and 2062. Each enclave is regulated and controlled by a specific corporation—though both verbs are used loosely. Miranda is conceived "miraculously," after her mother eats a durian fruit. Here, Lai represents another gender-queer conception and birth. This time, the female deity inhabits Miranda's mother. Miranda is born of two women. However, Miranda (think both "miracle" and *The Tempest*) is born with a persistent, "foul odour" (17) that smells like "cat piss" and just will not go away. Because of the smell, Miranda is ostracized during her entire childhood.

Eventually, the Ching family is expelled from Serendipity and forced to live in the Unregulated Zone. Outside Serendipity (read also: outside Eden), Miranda meets her own "salt fish girl" in Evie. Just as Nu Wa was attracted to the smell of the Salt Fish Girl, Miranda, the latest re-incarnation of Nu Wa, recognizes the fish smell in Evie. We eventually discover that Evie is one of a genetically engineered class of non-persons, designed solely for manual labor. These clones (called Sonias) are 0.3% carp. Evie says, "My genes are zero point three per cent *Cyprinus carpio*—freshwater carp. I'm a patented new fucking life form" (158). That three-tenths of a percent renders the Sonias (and the Miyakos type, cloned from cat cells) non-human. In "Future Asians," Lai notes that Evie and the Sonias were "Manufactured from the DNA of a Chinese-Canadian woman interned with her Japanese-Canadian husband during the Second World War, combined with the DNA of freshwater carp in order to get around human cloning laws" (175).

The Sonias and Miyakos are designed and created specifically for labor exploitation. And although they are closely monitored via a "Guardian Angel"—a biomechanical implant—some of them manage to escape and remove the Guardian Angel. The Sonias' house, protected by the durian tree, acts as a sort of perverse Garden of Eden, in which female refugees from Western techno-capitalism hide away and produce new Sonias, free from the Guardian Angel and from exploitation by global capital.

Salt Fish Girl queers the very nature of love and sex. The female creator deity Nu Wa shapes humans from yellow clay and gives them life. She gives them sex organs for pleasure; she later gives those organs a second purpose—reproduction. When they have sex, god averts her eyes so as not to shame them. In other words, she queers the entire Western, Judeo-Christian notion of the purpose of sex and human shame regarding sex. Later, Nu Wa takes physical form, motivated by desire for a woman. Nu Wa is a queer creator deity.

The form of reproduction is queered, as well. Miranda's conception is "miraculous." The Chings, Aimee and Stewart, believe that Miranda had been conceived because they had eaten a durian fruit from the Unregulated Zone. That much was true. However, they believed that it had been contaminated by rogue pollen (think Frankenstein's Monster unleashed into the world, uncontrollable). In fact, her conception was the result of Nu Wa inhabiting the seed of that durian fruit. An immaculate conception, between two women. Later, Miranda and Evie procreate, as well. After their first sexual encounter—out in the woods, out in nature—Miranda says, "it was at that moment that the child took root" (162). In the final scene of the book, the two find a salty hot spring. As they both enter the spring, Evie's legs fuse together (a mirror image of Nu Wa's legs splitting in chapter one), and Evie and Miranda entwine their bodies. As the scales emerge on Miranda's body, a small dark head emerges from just below her navel–another queer conception and birth.

While these two aspects queer the content of the book, Lai also queers the form of the book, in particular the form of science fiction. The ten chapters (though they do overlap at times) alternate between Nu Wa and Miranda, between mythology and science fiction. Nu Wa is a mythological creator god, who brings life to clay, who reincarnates as human, who travels to a city in the clouds, who inhabits a seed. These acts have no "scientific" explanation but carry the weight of a myth. As Joseph Campbell (he/him) said, myths may fail at a logical explanation of the world (by our Western standards), but they do explain the awe and wonder of the world. The Miranda chapters are rooted in an advanced Western techno-capital society. The ebook readers and manufactured clones all have "logical" explanations. And, yet, that too fails to explain the world. *Salt Fish Girl* brings both of these narratives, both these worldviews, both these understandings of what motivates and organizes the world, together. Maybe the world is larger—and more awesome—than either of these two systems can explain.

There are more things in heaven and Earth, Horatio,
Than are dreamt of in your philosophy.
(William Shakespeare, Hamlet, Act I, scene 5)

While Western science fiction is predicated on the extrapolation of changes in technology and society, many parts of the world, and many groups within the West, understand the world through other means. Their science is not the same as Western science. Scholars such as Grace Dillon (she/her), writers such as Nalo Hopkinson (she/her), Nnedi Okorafor (she/her), and Larissa Lai hope to expand our understanding of science and our expectations of science fiction.

Queer science fiction is here—get used to it.

8. Sex without Bodies

> *The communication satellite. The bank card. The laptop.*
> *The moon mission. Cyberspace. Virtual reality suits.*
> *Bioengineering. Cloning. Atomic weapons. Thin screens*
> *and smart paper. Hackers.... But is the End of Gender or a*
> *redefinition of sex on the list? No.*
> —Candace Jane Dorsey (she/her),
> "Some Notes on the Failure of Sex and Gender Inquiry
> in SF"

I REMEMBER THE early days of the internet. I first used it in the computer labs at university, and then at home with a dial-up modem. I distinctly remember the blip and hum of a dial-up modem, the monochrome green monitors, and the text-based screens (before the graphical browser). I recall the initial login to the WWW via an address at CERN in Switzerland, the static menu of areas on the web, numbered 1-8. They were heady days. It seemed as though the entire world had come online and was accessible. Jobs could be searched worldwide. Merchandise could be bought worldwide. People could congregate and talk worldwide. Then, as now, the talk often turned to sex.

Just five years later, Caitlin Sullivan (she/her) and Kate Bornstein (they/them) published *Nearly Roadkill: An Infobahn Erotic Adventure*. Sullivan has worked as a journalist and a playwright. Bornstein is a well-known performance artist and author. Bornstein's *Gender Outlaw*, a genderqueer autobiography and activist book, was a staple in Women's Studies classrooms for a while.

Bornstein and Sullivan met at a writer's conference. At the end of the conference, they exchanged snail mail addresses. People used to do that. At that point in time, Caitlin was using AOL, but Kate wasn't online at all. Once they were both online, they communicated via email. They had an idea for a book. They stored all (well, most of) their online adventures, their forays into chatrooms, and their discussion board logs. These stored chat longs became the central text of the novel. But, in many ways, the novel is a reflection of their own online interactions and experiences.

Mind you, in the early days, the internet was a different place. Oh, it was still dominated by sex, but it was all text-based. The first graphic browser (Mosaic) was released in 1993 and was overtaken by Netscape in 1995. In the essay "Will the Real Body Please Stand Up?" (1994), Sandy Stone (she/her) provides a succinct and informed history of the development of the internet, of cyberspace, and of online discussion boards.

In a rather naïve-sounding essay entitled "This Bridge Called My Mac," which appeared in *Off Our Backs*, emily lloyd (pronouns unknown) notes in 1995 that the internet is "a place where women can experiment with identity, communicate across state lines and generation gaps, discuss recent and age-old political issues in 'living forums,' and most importantly?…uh…flirt" (12). Lloyd notes that women can enter chatrooms under various screen names and take on a variety of personalities. In lloyd's case, lloyd is "tragically feminine" (12) and no one in Real Life will take lloyd seriously as a butch lesbian. Online, however, lloyd can transcend bodily identity and identifiers. Lloyd notes, "Online, identity can be a playground, rather than something fixed" (12) and that "Cyberspace forces us to question the concept of 'real identities'" (12).

Feminist and queer theorists have noted the ways in which too much of SF has failed to adequately represent sex, gender, and sexuality within its pages. Traditional western, patriarchal gender roles persist; males take on masculine roles and females take on feminine roles. Gay, lesbian, and transgender characters are often either absent or pathologized. So, Sullivan and Bornstein construct a novel that explores the possibilities of gender and sexuality within virtual space and simultaneously pushes at the boundaries of the SF novel.

The novel centers on five primary characters, all of whom are only ever known by their online screen names: Scratch, Winc, Toobe, Jabbathehut, and Gwynyth. The sixth character is a federal agent, Wally Budge—who turns out to be quite sympathetic. The premise of the story is that the federal government has been compelled by the Triumvirate Association of Business (TAB) to require every user of the internet to Register. The Registration process asks detailed questions about demographics, tastes, and spending habits. The agency then uses that information to send targeted ads at all users (which sounds rather a lot like Facebook). Because the TAB has largely funded the infrastructure of the Net, and since the Net has become an integral part of daily life and commerce, the TAB has threatened the government with a shutdown of the Net if it does not compel Registration. Any user who does not Register and any user who uses multiple online personas are in violation of the law. Wally Budge, an old-time, curmudgeonly beat cop who resists all things technological, works for the Federal Bureau of Census and Statistics, and is tasked with tracking down and apprehending scofflaws. Our heroes Scratch and Winc quickly become the public face of Registration Evasion.

Scratch and Winc are two individuals who spend a *lot* of time online, in a lot of different chatrooms, using a lot of different online identities. They are the TAB's and Budge's worst nightmare. The two individuals frequently bump into one another in chatrooms, and they frequently have cybersex—though they don't always know that they are together. Both Scratch and Winc have befriended a somewhat nerdy high-school-aged boy, Toobe. In altogether inappropriate behavior, they both send him transcripts of their online chats and sex sessions, and he also tracks them online.

Jabbathehut and Gwynyth are two cyber geniuses—a cyberwizard and a cyberwitch. They also have personal connections to Scratch and Winc, and, in the end, they bring their considerable technological skills to bear in rescuing Scratch and Winc.

Scratch and Winc have both resisted Registration, in part because it takes too long, in part because they hate the advertisements that are targeted to them, but primarily, they resist because of Question Three, which asks the user's sex. The question only provides two possible answers: male or female. Both Scratch and Winc refuse to reveal their sex and/or gender, even for a government form. They refuse to even lie about it for the purposes of registration. While they will assume and play a number of different sexes, genders, and sexualities online, they will never reveal their Real Life sex. But the government and the advertisers really, really want to know. Eventually, they call for an all-out, twenty-four-hour shutdown of the entire, global internet. As they call for the boycott, they make some strange allies, namely the NRA, and fail to persuade some seemingly logical allies, namely the Coalition of Lesbian, Gay, Bi, and Transsexuals.

Scratch and Winc begin their relationship in online chatrooms, specifically online sex chatrooms. They frequently engage in very graphically described sex acts. They seem drawn to one another; they seem to find one another despite the vastness of cyber space. They have heterosexual sex; they have homosexual sex; they have nonbinary sex. They have violent sex;

they have tender sex. And they have long discussions about the relationship of sex and gender. Both agree that biological sex is irrelevant and that gender is only a construct—one that is meant to be played with. They agree that the space of online chatrooms opens up a "third space" apart from the genders of "masculine" and "feminine." They enjoy the "fluidity" and the "performativity" of online identity. Although they are sometimes tempted to ask about the other's body (especially Scratch), they do not. For them, the sexed body and the performed gender are only one—quite fluid—aspect of the self. Most importantly, they understand that knowing the RL sex of the other would signal the end of the free play of imagination.

Four of the characters have struggled with gender in the Real World. Scratch and Winc both resist gender identification in the Real World, but they met a great deal of skepticism. We discover very late in the novel that Jabbathehut is a transwoman. In part because of the difficulty of that transition, Jabba has become a virtual (and I use that word advisedly) recluse. Gwyn, we also discover late in the novel, had spent much of her life in a freak show as the "bearded lady." When the freak show closed down, she, too, became a virtual recluse (with her many cats). From this perspective, they are both sympathetic to Scratch and Winc's own gender struggles.

As the crackdown on Evaders intensifies, the young Toobe is forced into hiding, and Scratch and Winc are forced out into the Real World. They have had a long online relationship, have had sex in a variety on online settings, but they know nothing about the physical bodies that the other inhabits. Winc writes to Scratch: "I've run down all the scenarios and realized it's fine whoever *you* are, I mean whoever you are is okay with me. But the idea of what each of *you* would make *me* is still tripping me out" (185-86). For Scratch and Winc, despite their insistence that their virtual selves are real, and despite their insistence that bodies do not matter, Winc suggests that the physical body is the *real* site of identity. Winc knows that "nothing about the content will change, but the form will be completely changed" (186). Unsurprisingly, then, when they physically meet, the relationship quickly disintegrates. Particularly for Scratch, the body overdetermines personal and sexual identity and undermines the possibilities of fluidity and play. Ze writes: "that hir face fixes hir permanently in time now, and ze can only be hirself, not Frankie, not the queerboy, not my fantasy of the week. Permanent" (220). For hir, only in the discorporate space of the chatroom can the relationship of body and identity slide freely, and only there can ze experience hir identity outside the confines of heteronormative binaries and sexualities.

Scratch, Winc, Jabba, and Gwynyth are all gender queer. They all reject, in one form or another, the traditional binary nomenclature and identities. While Jabba and Gwynyth have both absented themselves (as much as possible) from the Real World that rejects them, Scratch and Winc retreat from the Real World into a world of contingency, fluidity, and ether. Scratch and Winc, however, revel in the contingency of online identity. They use "identity tourism" as a means to discover a "real self," though it is a self that is not fixed, not stable, not unified, and not linked to any biological body or construct.

But, as Sandy Stone notes, until the technological singularity, that is, until the moment when we can all upload our identities into a machine and forsake the body for good, virtual identity remains attached to a corporeal body, for better or worse. Queer SF writers such as Sullivan and Bornstein offer us glimpses of worlds in which gender and sex are simply a string of zeros and ones in the ether.

9. Binary Queer

> *What was life without someone to love?*
> —Jennifer Marie Brissett, *Elysium*

IN HER CANONICAL—if controversial—essay, "The Five Sexes," medical researcher Anne Fausto Sterling (she/her) suggests that sex is not binary. Many of us in the late 20th-century West had been taught that all living things came in twos, whether by God or by natural reproductive processes. Sterling suggests that even though we try to put all human beings into one of two sex categories, we are actually working against nature when we do so. Nature does not do binaries. It is a rich set of possibilities that we then reduce to a binary pair due to our own beliefs/desires. Given that the belief in binary sex is so ingrained, how do we queer that idea? Jennifer Marie Brissett (she/her) has some ideas.

Brissett's *Elysium* is a short novel from Aqueduct Press that won a special citation for the Philip K. Dick Award in 2015. (I was on the jury that selected the awards that year.) Brissett is described as a "Jamaican-British American." Born in London, she moved to Cambridge, MA, when she was quite young. She was a computer programmer by training, but moved to Brooklyn to open an indie bookstore.

As Brissett notes in the afterword, she takes a bit of Roman history as source material. The Emperor Hadrian took a young lover, Antinous. After Antinous died (suicide, murder?), Hadrian built stuff—memorials—all over the place, including the Hadrian's Wall in northern England. The purpose of the wall was to keep out the barbarians. In Brissett's novel, the lovers Hadrian and Antinous transform into Adrian and Adrianne and Antoine and Antoinette—joined at times by Hector and Helen.

Brissett's novel takes a non-traditional form. As such, it's quite difficult to describe or summarize. The plot—the very point of the various scenes—does not become clear until the two-thirds mark. In the beginning, we're introduced to the characters Adrianne and Antoine, a woman and a man, married, though just barely. In the next section, Adrianne becomes Adrian, a gay man in a relationship with Antoine, who is dying. Adrian has a sexual relationship with Hector. They transform, again. Adrianne is in a relationship with the dying Antoinette. When she passes away, Helen swoops in to rescue Adrianne. We then meet Adrianne, a young acolyte in a cult of the virgin. When she takes a lover, Antoine, she is killed by the cult. Adrian awakens in a sanatorium, under observation for an attempted suicide. There, he meets Hector, a transwoman who has taken the name Helen. Antoine then rescues both Adrian and Hector, though they escape into a war-torn city. The characters morph again, now into two young boys, aged 12 and 14. Adrian and Antoine scrabble to survive in the war-torn city. After Antoine disappears, Adrian is rescued by his father—though he has been transformed by the dust "disease." But Adrian transforms into Adrianne. Her father is far along in the metamorphosis; she is just beginning to shift her shape. Another switch. Adrian fears for his wife Netta (short for Antoinette), as she is far along in her pregnancy. Adrian is the mastermind behind the underground city; living underground keeps them safe from the disease. He also has plans to build a ship and leave the Earth behind. The baby, Antoine, is born, though Netta dies. As in previous episodes, the loss of Netta devastates Adrian. An engineer has discovered a way to use the alien dust as an atmospheric coding system, which will be called Elysium, a memorial to the forgotten. Adrian wants

Antoine to board the ship and leave Earth. Instead, he gives his place to a woman with a young girl.

We finally meet the aliens who have brought the dust/disease, the Krestge. They have antlers and resemble elk. They have destroyed cities; they have undone the great memorials to love and humanity. We learn that the dust affects those with less melanin. People of color are more likely to survive. Humans are all gone; extinct. Only those who left Earth survive. We learn that hundreds of years later, a Krestge studying colonization has found the Elysium program, still running. However, the Krestge's attempt to "bridge" the program has caused some damage. And now the colonizer has damaged the only remaining legacy.

When Adrianne learns of the damage, learns that she can no longer see Antoine, she utters the phrase, "End Program."

As is often the case with experimental fiction, that (partial) summary does the book little justice. Brissett writes with style, with flare, with passion, and with conviction. The novel is multi-layered and multi-dimensional, inviting multiple readings.

But is it queer? I have discussed "queer" as a multivalent term, in which "queer" can refer to an identity, a sexuality or sex act, a way of setting things askew or challenging it, and as an interpretive lens.

The book does contain characters who identify as queer. Some times Adrian/Adrianne and Antoine/Antoinette are heterosexual; some times they are homosexual. Some times they engage in sex acts. Hector is almost always gay, except when Hector is trans. I suspect that the novel deliberately introduces us to Adrianne and Antoine first as a straight couple—and then queers them in the next section. The strategy compels the reader to now see them as queered. First as gay men, second as lesbians, and then as a vestal virgin, though she has a secret.

It's also true that the novel falls into the gay-best-friend trap. In a common Hollywood trope, the gay best friend ends up sacrificing themselves for the straight folks. Hector has been institutionalized, ostensibly for his grief following his mother's death—but really for being trans. So, when the Krestge move in, Hector sacrifices himself to allow Adrian and Antoine to get away—because "you saw the real me" (80). Nevertheless, *Elysium* does at least feature a transwoman.

The novel also seems to adopt the "love transcends all" trope. The Elysium program is based on Adrian and Netta. As the Krestge damage the program, we see the two lovers appear in all the different combinations. Adrian and Antoinette's love transcends sexed body, transcends gender, and transcends sexuality. In that sense, *Elysium* destigmatizes homosexuality. At the same time, it draws on the assimilationist argument of "love is love." While some in the LGBTQ community embrace "love is love" argument (particularly those in the same-sex marriage movement), many queers reject assimilating to cis-het norms and institutions.

The book also challenges some of the conventions of science fiction novels. Oh, very little is new under the sun (or green dot). Even so, the vast majority of novels—SF and otherwise—offer linear narratives and coherent characters. *Elysium* fragments the narrative and the characters. The narrative arc, such that there is one, is a spiral out from our Hadrian and Antinous. And although the characters, and events, and words curl back onto one another, they never quite cohere. Furthermore, the ending is less than triumphant, furthering queering the SF mode.

Elysium also seems to undercut the typical SF trope that technology will conquer all—no matter our troubles, science and tech will save the day. That trope is in the very origins of the genre. And, yet, each of the technological interventions fails. Oh, the humans hang on for a while. They live underground; they build rockets; they build their very own singularity machine among the stars—just as Hadrian remade the constellations for his lover. However, the military cannot stop the Krestge; the wall (an old technology) cannot keep them out; the mechanical wings cannot defeat them. The Elysium program, meant to memorialize humans, fails in the end. The Krestge damage it, and Adrianne ends it. Only the ships that leave succeed—maybe.

The novel also suggests that African Americans and People of Color take front and center in the future. The Krestge dust "discriminates." Those with little melanin are the first to succumb. Those with more melanin survive the dust—if not the war. All the technology, all the innovation is developed at the hands of people of color, subverting the prevalent Western stereotype. No white man saviors here. And yet, and yet, it all fails in the face of the colonizer. Even while three ships full of people of color head off to colonize another planet.

Since the central action in the novel is that the alien is trying to access the Elysium code, the novel features lines of binary code. Strings of zeroes and ones. (I ran the numbers through some binary translators and couldn't find any significance.) In other words, the book is literally a representation of the breakdown of the binary code. The binary fails. I would suggest that the book is less successful in breaking down the sex/gender binary code. The lovers tend to pair off—with occasional third complications. The lovers tend to manifest as either heterosexual or homosexual—with the complication of Hector. A random scrambling of the binary code of the Elysium program might have produced some even queerer combinations.

Brissett's take on the relationship between body and subject differs from what we saw in John Varley and Tanith Lee. Whereas they saw identity as something stable, as something independent of the physical body, Brissett shows it as a bit more malleable. Each iteration is a breakdown of a binary encoding. And, yet, because the new iterations are rooted in a binary system, they tend to recapitulate the very system they hope to break down.

10. Digital Memorials

ARE YOU READY for the singularity? Ready to abandon the meat and reside in the ether? Ready to become a string of ones and zeros? The promises of the singularity are many. Some hope to transcend the vicissitudes of the body. Getting old is not for the faint of heart. Some hope to "see" the wonders of the future. We saw examples of people trying to hold on just long enough to see the Mueller Report! Some hope to explode the relationship between body and subjectivity. They cannot be defined by their body if they don't have one. Others, like Gabriela Damián Miravete (she/her), imagine another use for a virtual digital presence.

Miravete published "And They Will Dream in the Garden" in *Latin American Literature Today* (2018), in both Spanish and English (translation by Adrian Demopulos [she/her]). The short story was the 2019—and, I suppose, the very last—recipient of the James Tiptree Award. It became the Otherwise Award the following year. (I had the honor to serve on the jury that selected Miravete's story as the winning entry.) In May 2019, Miravete attended WisCon to be crowned (tiaraed, more precisely) and to receive her prize—a lot of chocolate. As Miravete talked about her motivations and goals for writing the story, she and many of us in the audience were moved to tears.

Since 1993, hundreds of women have been murdered, especially in the Juárez region of México. Initially, the police were entirely apathetic about the murders. They simply did not care. They did not investigate. As the numbers grew, as internal and external pressure grew, the murders became more visible. They have been written about (see Alicia Gaspar de Alba's (she/her) novel *Desert Blood* and Stella Pope Duarte's (she/her) novel *If I Die in Juárez*) and sung about (see Tori Amos's (she/her) "Juarez" and Los Tigres del Norte's "Mujeres de Juárez"). At least two feature films (Backyard [El Traspatio], and *Bordertown*) were based on the murders; at least four documentaries have been made (*Blood Rising, Señorita Extraviada, Equal Means Equal, Bajo Juárez: La ciudad devorando a sus hijas*). Miravete's short story joins these texts.

I'm not wholly certain that "And They Will Dream in the Garden" is a queer text. Not in the way that other entries in this book have been. It does not feature queer characters struggling with their identity—as Kate Bornstein and Caitlin Sullivan's *Roadkill* does (see Shade 8). It does not feature queer communities in some imagined future—as Janelle Monáe's *Dirty Computer* does (see Shade 12). It does not feature gender fluidity—as Jennifer Brissett does (see Shade 9). But as I noted in earlier chapters, both science fiction and queer studies look to future societies, what they might look like, and how we might achieve them. So, too, does "They Will Dream in the Garden."

I suggest that the Garden in "They Will Dream in the Garden" accomplishes two things, not necessarily at the same time. The Caretaker and the apprentice Teachers welcome children into a beautiful garden filled with orange trees and flowers. The Garden is a memorial, a monument to the murdered women. They now exist as fully interactive holograms. Marisela, the Caretaker, studied computer science specifically to create the holograms as memorials. But when Dulce, a close friend, is murdered, Marisela alters the mission and purpose of the Garden. It now teaches an entire generation "that there are alternatives to violence" (2018), that they must not touch someone without consent. The Mexican youth are required by law to come to the Garden, to learn the lessons of the new generation.

And, so, the program has worked. In this imagined México, crime has diminished. The number of murdered women has diminished. And, yet, Marisela knows that it is not enough. Marisela continues to work on the technology, to give the holograms the ability to dream at night, when the children have gone home.

In this way, Miravete imagines how we might bring about a new society in which women cannot go missing without anyone caring, in which women are not seen as subhuman, in which everyone has the chance to fulfill their dreams, in which those whose dreams were cut short can dream on.

The story opens with an epigraph, a to-do list, a list of things that a woman had intended to do with her life, a list of things undone, a list by a woman who was murdered. Within the story, the Caretaker hopes to be able to give the dead women the ability to fulfill their dreams. And when the crowds of young children go home, they can dream in their lovely Garden. They can do what had been taken away from them. Further, writing the story *performs* the story. Miravete creates a memorial to the women; then she offers a way to reshape our future society.

11. Hermaphrodites in Space

> *The thinking that you can only be male or female went out with the twentieth century. Since bigenderism exists as a choice, it's hardly surprising that someone had the idea to integrate both sexes into one body.*
> —Sayuri Ueda, *The Cage of Zeus*

IN 4 BCE, Ovid (he/him) wrote his Metamorphoses, including the story of Hermaphroditus and Salmacis. The story provides an origin tale for both the narcissus flower and for hermaphrodites—those whose body is both male and female. For centuries, that story provided the term we used to describe individuals whose body was neither female nor male, or both male and female. By the 19th century, medical discourse had defined several kinds of hermaphrodites. While in some cultures hermaphrodites were seen as blessed or holy, in the West, they were largely ridiculed and shunned. Consequently, usage of the term was replaced by a more neutral and less historical term, intersex. In 2005, fifty leading experts on intersex conditions issued a consensus statement, suggesting a change in nomenclature to "Disorders of Sexual Development" (Vilain et al.).

In 2004, Sayuri Ueda (上田早夕里) (she/her) published *The Cage of Zeus*. Born in Kobe, Hyōgo Prefecture in 1964, Ueda is a well-known SF writer in Japan. Her work has won multiple awards, including the Komatsu Sakyo Award for her first novel, *Mars Dark Ballade*; her collection *Fin and Claw* was nominated for the Japan SF Award; and her novel *The Ocean Chronicles* won the Best SF prize in 2010.

The novel is set in a future in which humans have colonized the moon and Mars. After a number of generations, Mars has finally become comfortably habitable. However, humans hope to move even farther out into space. They currently have several outposts at Jupiter. In this future world, presumably, gender and sexual identity are understood to be fluid, and yet, gender biases persist. The basic premise of the novel is that the government has created a group of hermaphrodites to form a non-gendered, and therefore, non-discriminatory, society. The so-called Rounds now live in a secluded environment on a space station orbiting Jupiter largely for their own protection. Not everyone appreciates or accepts the Rounds. Much of the population of Earth and Mars fears or distrusts the Rounds. They're afraid they'll "catch" hermaphroditism, apparently. Others see them as a threat. They're "weird" and "strange" and a "collective" and they'll take over. And so a religious group, The Vessel of Life, wants to wipe them out. They see the Rounds as an abomination. They blackmail a terrorist, Karina Majella, into carrying out their plot. On the station Jupiter-1, the Rounds live within the Special District, with limited contact with the other scientists and crew. The Rounds call the crew "Monaurals" because they are limited to one sex.

I'll not spoil the mystery. I'll not say whether the plot succeeds or fails. You'll have to read it to find out. However, *Cage of Zeus* does offer a queered society. The Rounds, at least in theory, seem to have a wholly queered sex and sexuality. They suggest that their bodies are different from the rest of humanity; their sexuality is different from the rest; and their reproduction is (somewhat) different.

As a work of SF, the novel is uneven (many of my students called it "painful"). It contains a number of "infodumps"—large sections of background information dumped onto the reader. In one case, Ueda provides background information on how the Rounds were created and details of their physiology.

In another place, Ueda provides a long section on the differences between sex and gender. While that information might be useful to a casual reader, it certainly was not necessary for those in my class. It's also consistent with Ueda's afterword in which she notes that she had recently learned about, and was interested in studying more about, intersexuals.

And, to be sure, the book has other shortcomings. Even though it offers the Rounds as a utopian ideal to single-sexed bodies and gender discrimination, it does not succeed in breaking out of sexual binaries and cisgender. While the station director, Liezel Kline, suggests that the psyche of the Rounds is different from that of the Monaurals. The leader of the Rounds, Fortia, also suggests that they simply think differently about themselves, their bodies, and their sexuality. In reality, they remain mired in thinking about the "female part" of their identity or the "male part" of their bodies. For example, when the Round Veritas and the Monaural Harding enter into a relationship, Harding can only love Veritas as a woman (emotionally, physically). When Veritas wants to love Harding "as a man," Harding is repelled. Furthermore, the Rounds remain binary in their pairings. The argument is that each Round has a penis and vagina, and during sex, each penetrates (or can penetrate) the other simultaneously. Even if Rounds do engage in sex this way, it needn't mean that they would have to form pairs. Yet, the Rounds still pair off in somewhat normative families, with two partners giving birth to shared children.

Furthermore, the Monaural side of the station does not reflect the diversity of gender and sexuality that supposedly exists on Earth and Mars. One early infodump notes that gender has become quite fluid and that people change their sex back and forth fairly easily. And, yet, not one gender fluid or trans individual seems to exist on the entire space station. If gender fluidity is a commonplace as the characters suggest, then we would likely see one or more gender-fluid individuals in the novel.

Nevertheless, I suggest the book works well in several ways. First, it captures the likely mistrust and backlash at sexual and gender experimentation. We needn't look far to see that that would be a likely outcome. We see the political and physical violence all around us aimed at nonbinary and gender-nonconforming people. On November 2019 Transgender Day of Remembrance, the website *TransRespect* reported that 331 "trans or gender-diverse" people had been killed in the last calendar year, with a total of 3314 killed worldwide since TDoR began in 2008. But the novel offers a variety of responses within the Monaurals beyond overt terrorism and violence. Some Monaurals eagerly welcome the Rounds while others are more ambivalent. In other words, the responses to change are varied and complex.

Second, it acknowledges sexual diversity. It puts hermaphrodites front and center in the novel. In a linguistically necessary strategy, the translator of the novel uses non-gendered Spivak pronouns for the Rounds (ey, em, eir), signaling their sexual and gendered difference from the Monaurals. Furthermore, the novel demonstrates the tensions between group identity and conformity and with individual identity and dissention. While the Rounds live in identical housing and wear identical robes, several of the characters illustrate that they are not all the same. They are not at all like the Borg collective. We discover that the Round Lanterna was born with both sets of genitalia, but in an unusual formation, rendering em marginal to the other Rounds. Because of this difference, Lanterna takes a non-Round name, Tei, and works as an intermediary between Rounds and Monaurals. However, Tei worries that eir genitalia variation is simply another natural variation, and that others like em will follow, potentially creating still another binary, and still another point of discrimination. Here, Tei's concern and argument echoes the contemporary discourse around intersexuals.

Another Round, Tenebrae, has no desire to remain with the Rounds. Ey finds eir life too regimented and too determined. Ey knows that they will all, eventually, leave Jupiter to explore space. Ey has no interest in that. Ey leaves the Round community, undergoes surgery to become a Monaural with a single sex. Tenebrae becomes Barry Wolfson and lives and works among the Monaurals. Barry suggests that other Rounds feel the same way and would like to follow him into Monaural life. In this way Ueda avoids one of the traps of SF—a monolithic utopian society. Here, the experiment to end gender discrimination fails. The repressed sexuality returns, just in another form. Tenebrae/Wolfson's monaural sexuality was repressed in Round society, though it finds its expression in monarual society.

In an Afterword, Ueda notes that she wants to write about intersexed individuals and about gender-diverse people more, especially in non-SF work. I hope that she does. As for *Cage of Zeus*, I do think Ueda complicates many of the issues in interesting ways. The presentation, however, is at times a bit naïve. What *The Cage of Zeus* demonstrates, what the 2005 conference on Pediatric Endocrinology shows, and what the everyday lived experiences of intersex individuals reveals is that we are far from finished thinking through questions of embodiment, nomenclature, and discrimination.

12. Janelle Monáe's Queer America

I'm not America's nightmare
I am the American dream (Oh-oh, oh-oh, oh-oh, oh-oh)
Just let me live my life.
—Janelle Monáe, "Crazy, Classic Life"

"AMERICA'S NIGHTMARE" IS an expression that has been used many times in US history. It was used to describe the US involvement, and no apparent way out of, the conflict in Vietnam. Later, the expression was plastered on the front pages of newspapers following 9/11. And, most recently, the expression has been employed in the wake of the United States' exit from Afghanistan.

In 1964, Malcolm X (he/him) gave a speech in which he said, "I don't see an American dream. I see an American nightmare." In 1967, Dr. Martin Luther King (he/him) offered his "dream" for America, though three years later, he would say that the "dream" was a "nightmare." He meant that his optimism was a bit naïve; he meant that the racism was more ingrained and more institutionalized than he had thought.

In 2018, Janell Monáe offered her own commentary on the nightmare.

Janelle Monáe Robinson (she/her) was born in Kansas City. Her parents were working class. Monáe aspired to be an artist and moved to New York City at a relatively young age. She released her first EP at age 18.

To be sure, Monáe has consistently worked in the science fiction mode, from her retelling of Fritz Lang's (he/him) 1927

Metropolis to her alter ego, Cindy Mayweather, the android (Sandifer). All of her work up to *Dirty Computer* featured Mayweather the android. *DC* is the first work in which she drops the android persona and offers a glimpse into the "real" Janelle Monáe. The songs are filled with bits and pieces of Monáe's personal biography.

In her earlier works, she had used the "android" as a symbol for the Other, for those on the margins, those forgotten by society. Her use of the figure of the android differs from other writers such as Philip K. Dick, who saw the android as a symbol of those who had lost their humanity. Instead, Monáe (or Cindy Mayweather) identified as an android. She noted in a 2010 interview with *Rolling Stone* that she only dated androids (Hoard).

In the new work, that android takes a new form—the dirty computer. Those whose programming has been "corrupted," those who do not conform to societal norms, are called "dirty computers." And, so, they must be "cleaned." Difference must be erased; memories must be wiped.

The videos here are filled with "dirty computers": women, women of color, queer women and men, queers. *Dirty Computer* dropped roughly the same time as *Black Panther* (*BP* on 02/16/18 and *DC* on 4/27/18). Monáe has noted how important that film was to her—and to communities of color—to see themselves represented; to see themselves represented en masse; to see black and African cultures and clothing and language featured prominently was awe-inspiring. *Dirty Computer* has both a similar effect and a similar aim. I suspect that more people have seen *BP* than have seen *DC*, but it doesn't matter. It *is* being seen. By large numbers. And it is affecting viewers and up-and-coming artists. Like Octavia Butler before her, Monáe has lamented that she never saw herself in science fiction. Like Ryan Coogler, she consciously wanted to change that.

Shade 12

To some extent, *Dirty Computer* partakes in an assimilationist argument about PoC and queers. The first song of the movie (the song tracks differ between album and film) is "Crazy, Classic Life." In this piece, Monáe sings that she is not a "nightmare" but an embodiment of the "American Dream." She wants all the same things as everyone else: to have friends, to party, to have a "classic life." Some queer scholars would call this the "politics of respectability." But that's not quite it.

In "Django Jane," Monáe refers to the 2012 film by Quentin Tarantino, *Django Unchained*. Instead of the well-worn plot in which a man is motivated to seek revenge by the loss of his woman, however, Monáe undertakes the task herself. Indeed, she tells men "you were not involved." But she offers solidarity with women, invoking Fem the Future and Black Girl Magic. She queers her gender solidarity by claiming "we gon' start a motherfuckin' pussy riot," a reference to the Russian activist and musical group jailed by Putin. Monáe's movement, her solidarity, does not constitute another "wave" of feminism, but a "tsunami."

In "Pynk," Monáe invokes the aforementioned pussy power, lyrically and visually. Janelle/Jane and her friends inhabit the Pynk Restaurant, where "girls eat free and never leave." Her entourage wears pink dresses that resemble labia. As the dancers open their legs/labia, Monáe sings: "Pynk, like the inside of your... baby." When Zen (Tessa Thompson [she/her]) appears between Monáe's legs, it signals either a sex act, or a rebirth. They have found their identity, their community, and their paradise.

Monáe wants to expand—to queer—what the "classic life" is. She expands what the American Dream is. Near the beginning of the film, in the midst of the song, "Crazy, Classic Life," Monáe interweaves a recording of Martin Luther King (he/him) reading from the Declaration of Independence, noting that the reality of that Declaration has not lived up to the promise of the American Dream. The film ends with the song, "Americans," which further expands the notion of what American is. It is not Donald Trump's America. Nor white supremacists', nor MAGAts'. It is MLK's America. It is Janelle Monáe's America. It is a queered America.

"Please sign your name on the dotted line."

13. *Sense8*, Queering the Family, and the Collective

> *I realized quickly when I knew I should*
> *That the world was made up of this brotherhood of man*
> *For whatever that means*
> —4 Non Blondes, "What's Up"

WHAT WAS IT that Plato said about the cave? In his intellectual exercise, the individuals chained to the wall of the cave watch shadows flickering on the wall in front of them. For them, they are watching reality, unaware that anything else exists outside these shadows on the wall. But the philosopher is freed from the chain and hopes to learn of the higher levels of reality. The ideal would be to perceive the world as it is—even if that is never possible. The Wachowskis explored similar ideas in the *Matrix* (1999—) film franchise.

Sense8 was a bit of a phenomenon when it began airing in 2015. It garnered attention because it was created by the creators of *The Matrix* trilogy (the Wachowskis). It was created by two trans women. One of the principle leads was a trans woman. And it featured lots of beautiful people having sex. The series was cancelled after two seasons, putatively because of the enormous production costs. Filming an all-star cast in eight locations around the world does not come cheap. *Sense8* offered enormous potential. Like so many other things with so much riding on it, it just did not live up to the hype.

Oh, it was queer. It featured queer directors and writers, queer actors, and queer characters. Furthermore, it featured (some) queer storylines, from Pride week in San Fran, to a confrontation with Trans-Exclusionary Radical Feminists, from unaccepting parents, to enforced surgeries. It also queered the notion of family, with a variety of blood and chosen families. Sometimes blood family works, sometimes it does not. Sometimes chosen family works, sometimes it does not. None of these things is trivial.

But the queerness of the sensate family does not hold up. Most of the sensates have bio-fam issues. Wolfgang had a criminal father who derided him; Nomi has a mother who rejects her identity and name; Kala has a fiancé and father-in-law who are corrupt; Bak Sun has a father who rejects her over his son. Capheus has a mother dying of AIDS; Will has a tough-as-nails cop father who rejects his willingness to save a gangbanger, while Riley is estranged from her father in Iceland. Perhaps their familial issues have made them candidates to become sensates. As their new family becomes activated and integrated, they discover that these new family members do not lie to them; they discover that they have their back; they discover that they support them; they discover that they love them (physically, emotionally). So, yes, *Sense8*—as queer communities have long done—queers the nature and function of a family. It does not, however, translate much into personal identity or sexual identity.

The group sex scenes suggest a kind of familiarity, a kind of intimacy not possible elsewhere. They also show eight people engaged in sex with one another. While the show does not feature any non-binary characters, it does feature fluidity in sexual practice. But that fluidity does not appear to be foundational, does not appear to transfer outside the sensate group. In other words, loving others of both sexes, and making love to others of both sexes, has not fundamentally altered their sexual identity. *Sense8* would have fundamentally queered identity, sexuality, and family, I believe, if it had extended desire and sex beyond the sensate group.

Sense8 also had an issue with race. Yes, it purported to be a racially diverse cast. It features a storyline set in Nairobi, though played by a British actor (Aml Ameen [he/him]). But Capheus is the only one of the eight sensates who lives in squalor. The Capheus storyline adheres to the common Western stereotypes about Africans. Yes, *Sense8* features an Indian woman (Tina Desai [she/her]), a practicing Hindu. However, the Kala storyline also adheres to a stereotypical notion of Indian women: passive, demure, sexually reserved, devout. It also features "loving" men in her life who are, ultimately, corrupt. The series features a South Korean woman (Doona Bae [she/her]), who is quite accomplished. However, the Bak Sun storyline also plays on stereotypes of the patriarch who will not accept his daughter, even though she outshines her brother in every way. But her dying mother makes her promise to take care of her brother. Yes, it features a Mexican man (Miguel Ángel Silvestre [he/him]) who is a famous actor. However, the Lito story features a closeted gay man within hypermasculine Mexican society. Furthermore, in a country that is predominantly mestizo, Lito is played by a light-skinned Spaniard.

The remaining four sensates are white Nomi Marks (Jamie Clayton [she/her]), Riley Gunnarsdóttir (Tuppence Middleton [she/her]), Wolfgang Bogdanow (Max Reimelt [he/him]), and Will Gorski (Brian J. Smith [he/him]). According to Wikipedia, in 2018, only 11.5% of the world's population was white. If sensates are chosen randomly, it would seem mathematically unlikely that fully half the family would be white. Was that choice racial bias? What that choice marketing? Was that choice budgetary (in terms of travel and filming and actors)? Regardless of the rationale, the representation and the optics are not good.

I think it is also arguable that the white characters are also stereotypes. In some sense, all eight of the sensates are comic characters. Will's white cop with a big heart, Nomi's misunderstood hacker, and Wolfie's transcendence of his abusive father are stereotypes, too. But I would respond with two points. For one, since white characters really do see much more complicated representations, when they are reduced to a stereotype, it causes less harm. And on the flip side of that, characters of color rarely escape such stereotyped representations. And that perpetuates the myth that that is all there is to them. I am quite certain that some Korean women have lived through experiences similar to that lived through by Bak Sun. But that is all we see; we do not get to see the wide range of possible lived experiences for a Korean woman.

In re-watching the series, one of the central questions for me was, what do the sensates represent? What were the Wachowskis trying to get at in their creation? What cultural need or gap do the sensates fill? In *Old Futures* (2018), Alexis Lothian suggests that they address a yearning for spaces of public sex that the queer communities have lost. I would suggest that the sensates also address the notion of the individual versus the collective. At each moment in our history, we have wrestled with this idea. Here in the United States, we have vacillated between rugged individualism and collective action. The 1960s saw a turn toward a collective consciousness, while the 1980s saw us turn back toward individualism.

I think we are on the crux of another change in our attitudes about the community, about collectivity. We are seeing, *especially* among younger citizens, the damage done to our society and our planet by individualism. They recognize that we need to come together to address these issues, to address these injustices. They recognize that we are greater together than the sum of our parts. Shows like *Sense8* queer our notions of subjectivity, of individualism, of family, of love, and of sex.

I wish that *Sense8* had done a better job of representing that ideal, but I do think it pointed us in that direction.

14. A Bridge Cemented in Blood

> *The true focus of revolutionary change is never merely the oppressive situations which we seek to escape, but that piece of the oppressor which is planted deep within each of us.*
> Audre Lorde, "Age, Race, Class, and Sex"*

IN 1969, URSULA K. Le Guin (she/her) published *The Left Hand of Darkness*. By that point in time, Le Guin had published four novels (three in the Hainish SF series and one in the Earthsea fantasy series) and eight short stories. But this one won both the Hugo Award and the Nebula Award for best novel—the first time that had ever happened.

Le Guin was the daughter of Theodora Kroeber (she/her, writer) and Alfred Kroeber (he/him, anthropologist). As many a student has noted, the novel reads like an anthropologist or sociologist might have written it. Not exactly a fair criticism, by my lights, but I can see their point.

According to Le Guin herself, the novel was a scientific experiment. She posited a hypothesis: what would a society look like if the inhabitants had no (permanent) sex? How might it affect gender? Familial structures? Government, politics, war? Reproduction? Like any scientist, she set that idea in motion, and constructed the frozen world of Gethen.

The planet Gethen is occupied by human descendants (or antecedents) adapted to a very cold climate. For 42 years, scientists from the Ekumen (a loose conglomeration of other

---

* Thanks to the amazing Lysa Rivera for reminding me of this quote.

human-inhabited planets) studied the planet and wrote reports before sending a single envoy, Genly Ai, to the planet. He lives among the Gethenians, studies them, and tries to convince them to join the Ekumen. Nearly all the Gethenians distrust him, except for the king's counsel, Estraven. But for deeply misogynistic reasons, Ai distrusts Estraven.

Apart from the extreme cold, the lack of game animals, the lack of flying animals, and the lack of war, the most salient feature of the planet is that the inhabitants have no permanent sex. Most of their lives, they are unsexed; they have no sex organs, a state which they call *somer*. However, they regularly go into *kemmer*, the state in which their sex organs develop and they can engage in sex and reproduction. They do not know, however, which sex organs will develop. Although which sex organs develop depend on environmental and social factors, any given person might be female one month and male the next. That person might impregnate someone one time, and might be impregnated the next.

The effects of that, it would seem, are profound. As a scientist, Le Guin provides field reports on Gethen, folk tales and myths, and other background material for understanding Gethen. In Ong Tot Oppong's field notes, she writes of these social differences. According to Oppong, Gethenians have no preference for male or female when they enter *kemmer*. Can you imagine? Is that feasible in a patriarchal and sexist society? In the United States in the late '60s, and in the United States today, being female has enormous consequences—social, political, personal, financial. On Gethen, none of that is true. No wage gap. No glass ceiling. No sexual assault. Completely different perspectives on childbearing and childrearing. None of the consequences of gender that we see. Oppong notes that, on Gethen, individuals are not seen as "masculine" or "feminine" but, rather, "One is respected and judged only as a human being. *It is an appalling experience*" (94) [emphasis added]. Indeed, we are so accustomed to these biases, these social norms, that the idea of "giving them up" can be appalling. Through this device, Le Guin signals that Genly Ai, our "eye" into Gethenians and a genderless society, brings our biases to the planet Gethen.

So, Genly continues to see Gethenians as women and as men, and it takes over a year and a harrowing experience crossing the Gobrin Ice sheet for him to begin to see the Gethenians as something other than women and men. The only term he has for this third gender is "manwoman." Nevertheless, he comes to love deeply this "manwoman."

While I love the novel, and my students generally did, too, it is far from perfect. Le Guin has been criticized for her use of the masculine universal pronoun "he" to describe the Gethenians. While she initially defended her choice, she later recanted and agreed that the story would have worked better had Genly used gender neutral pronouns to describe the Gethenians. Consider: the Gethenians are neither male nor female, neither woman nor man. And, yet, Ai can only see them that way. Because he is from Earth, because he holds views about sex and gender from the late 1960s, he sees masculine as the universal and as the preferable. He always views any sign of the feminine (as *he* sees it; "feminine" makes no sense to Gethenians) with disgust or suspicion. But as readers, Ai's viewpoint is our view on the Gethenians, and his perspectives shape our own. I suspect that this was less of an issue in 1969 than it is in 2021. Readers' views of gender in 1969 were closer to Ai's than ours are today. My students today have a hard time getting past Ai's misogyny and don't understand the "universal" masculine "he." However, at the same time, reading *Left Hand* today demonstrates the importance of pronouns. We see how thoroughly Ai's use of "he" determines our view of Estraven. It makes a strong case for gender neutral pronouns.

In addition, Le Guin does not explore the range of sexualities on Gethen. The scientific reports acknowledge that people exist who predetermine which sex they will be during *kemmer*. They are viewed as perverts. The reports also note that some Gethenians will be with someone of the same sex, though they are called "half-dead" and marginalized in Gethenian society. We know that human sexuality is varied and multiple. If the Gethenians are of the same stock as humans, then it is likely that they would have a variety of sexualities, as well. For one, Le Guin suggests that the severe climate of Gethen shapes and limits some human practices. So, *maybe*, but probably not sexual desire. She also focuses here on the reproductive features of the *somer/kemmer* system. Human sexuality, however, is about much more than reproduction, and Le Guin makes little space for non-reproductive sex on Gethen. And, yet, for readers in 2021, it is a hard conceit to accept. Here, too, Le Guin has noted that she should have made space for a more varied sexuality.

Audre Lorde suggests that simply changing regimes is not enough. Simply ending oppressive situations or structures is not enough. She argues that we must also confront and eliminate the hint of the oppressor within us. For Lorde, we must throw off the old ways of thinking that reside within us. Ai tries, over time, to expel those internalized beliefs that he brings to Gethen—with some success. Lorde's argument may seem to be at odds with Le Guin's dualism, in which "Light is the left hand of darkness, and darkness the right hand of light" (222). A bit of the other is in you; a bit of you is in the other. I would suggest that *The Left Hand of Darkness*, Le Guin, and Lorde all want us to see the human in the other. But they also want us to expel that which prevents us from seeing the other as fully human.

The novel begins with a scene in which the King of Karhide, Argaven, ceremonially completes a new bridge by cementing the keystone. Estraven explains that keystones were once set with mortar mixed with the blood of a human sacrifice. In the logic of the narrative, then, Estraven cements the bridge between Gethen and the Ekumen with his own blood, his own sacrifice. This metaphor seems to apply to all those who have come before in the fight for recognizing gender differences, in the fight for acknowledging sexual difference. For my students today, their understanding of gender and sexuality, their everyday lived experiences are made possible by those who came before them. Not that they willingly sacrificed themselves as Estraven did, but their lives did matter. May we recognize in Estraven's cementing the bridge of understanding with his own life the path laid down by those who came before us.

15. Queer Muslims in Space

> *I also want to see more intersectionality and exploration of the complexity of our lives. Queer Muslims, Non-binary people of faith, couples (or polyamorous) relationships that don't center white people.*
> —Craig L. Gidney in Mandelo, "Queering SFF"

IN THE INTRODUCTION, I argued that 2010 marked a sort of turning point for Queer SF. Discussions about origin stories and ur-texts will only get one so far, so I have no interest in pointing to a particular author or text or publication. But it was around 2010 when we began to see more SF stories by queer writers, more stories about queer characters and content, and more stories that queered readers' expectations of what SF is and should do. To bolster this point, I point to a roundtable discussion moderated by Lee Mandelo. Published in 2020, it asks queer SF writers what has changed in SF publishing in the past ten years. Their answer: "a lot."

The year 2011 saw the publication of two notable pieces: "To Follow the Waves" by Amal el-Mohtar (she/her) and "God in the Sky" by An Owomoyela (se/ses/sem). El-Mohtar is a writer, poet, and reviewer, who grew up in Canada and Lebanon. She currently lives in Glasgow. Owomoyela did undergraduate work in Iowa largely in linguistics. Se now lives in the Bay Area.

The beautifully written "To Follow the Waves" features Hessa, the daughter of a poet and a mathematician, who is recruited to the relatively new craft of recording dreams into crystals. The purchaser then experiences the dream through the crystal. When Hessa receives a commission for a new dream that falls outside her own experience, she struggles. She has been asked to construct a dream of a woman with a much younger man in the ocean waves. Hessa has never seen the ocean, and she knows little of passion and desire. However, a chance encounter with a woman (Nahla) in a café provides her with her inspiration for the dream.

The sources of her desire for the stranger are complicated. The thing that attracts her initially is the fact that Nahla wears her hair loose and flowing. Hessa notes that women wear their hair tied up in braids, and that the patterns of the braids signify what trade they are associated with. This woman is either unaffiliated or refuses to publicly signify her status. Hessa is also attracted to her bravery in wearing her hair unbound and her willingness to risk the stares and disapprobation. Finally, Hessa is drawn to her sexually. She finds that she cannot stop thinking of her, and the stranger becomes the basis of her dream commission.

Something unusual happens, though. Nahla becomes aware of the dreams, aware that she is the source of them, aware that other people are experiencing this intense desire for her. She confronts Hessa for this intrusion into her life, for appropriating her without consent. They begin the process of getting to know one another as people, not just as objects of fantasy.

The story takes place in Dimashq (Damascus), the capital city of Syria. Hessa also mentions the Al-Zahiriyya Library, which is located in Damascus. Set in a predominantly Muslim country, the focus on the hair serves as analog for the public mandates regarding hair and head coverings. Hessa finds Nahla's rejection of those social norms enticing. Furthermore, her same-sex desire for Nahla similarly stands outside social norms.

The technology of the dream crystals allows Hessa to experience her desire for Nahla in the privacy of her home.

Nahla, the brave one, finds Hessa and wants to explore the relationship in a (more) public space and on equal footing.

"God in the Sky" features Katrina, the daughter of a teacher and an activist, who is a graduate student. When a strange phenomenon appears in the sky, the world is thrown into chaos, as is Katrina's life. Her research department shuts down, her father jumps on a plane to find his estranged ex-wife, her girlfriend Josey heads back to Tennessee to see family, and her grandfather returns to Islam.

Katrina is a person of science; she makes sense of the world through the discourses of math and logic. When the light appears in the sky, she takes refuge in the math. She knows that the full effects of the light will not touch Earth for at least another twenty years, if at all. She also knows that the universe is vast, and we do not understand most of it. So, for Katrina, it is perplexing how people are responding to the light in the sky. A mayor has called it "God." That religious turn, in part, catalyzes her grandfather's return to Islam.

He notes that he had been Muslim when he grew up in Egypt and that he had drifted away over the years. But in this moment of uncertainty, he finds the verities of religion to be comforting. For him, that means Arabic and Islam. As in the book/film *Contact* (Carl Sagan [he/him]/Robert Zemekis [he/him]), "God in the Sky" juxtaposes two approaches to the world, two discourses through which we make sense of the world we live in. Katrina does not understand her grandfather's turn to religion, and she tries to "educate" him as they look up at the sky. And, yet, for him, that only leads back to the awesome power (*agape*) of God. For all her bravado, though, and for all her complaints about other people's turn to family and loved ones, she, too, needs familial contact in the end.

However, for me, the queerest element of the story is its unrelenting ambivalence, its uncertainty, its unwillingness to resolve the conflict. We have (largely) learned our expectations for what texts—including SF texts—are supposed to do. They frequently pose a problem, work through conflict, and arrive at a resolution. Not here. Every element of the story is left unresolved: will she finish her graduate work? Will her father find her mother? Will her girlfriend return from Tennessee? Will her grandfather immerse himself in Islam? Will the light in the sky swallow up the Earth? Owomoyela refuses all those expectations.

Both stories feature (if not center) queer characters and queer desire; both stories center Muslim communities and individuals. Both stories dramatize the relationship between faith and science. They are examples of the turn to wider representation in SF (just prior to the Sad Puppies and perhaps a predicate to them). They center the lives and loves of people underrepresented in SF. And, most importantly, they are examples of how much these wider horizons enrich the field of SF. And inasmuch as SF is about thinking through the human condition, they are lovely and necessary additions to the conversation.

16. Recentering Life in *Salt Fish Girl* (redux)

IN HIS ESSAY "Philosophy and the Future of Fiction" (1980), William Gass (he/him) notes that one takes "a lifetime to read" the work of James Joyce (he/him). Indeed, many scholars have dedicated their careers to Joyce and to *Ulysses*. Joyce himself was reputed to have said that his *Finnegans Wake* could (should?) take the place of the experience of life. To my knowledge, Larissa Lai has made no such claim, and yet, she has produced a text so rich in detail, so subtle in nuance that it may well rise to that level. All of which is a long way to say that no simple or easy essay is going to do the novel justice. As with Joyce's novels, Lai's novel bears rich, pungent fruit with each reading. Rereading is highly recommended.

Salt Fish Girl features two intertwining (I choose that word deliberately) narratives. We begin with a retelling and reframing of the Chinese creation story of Nu Wa and Fu Xi. In one version of the myth, Nu Wa created human beings out of clay, and Fu Xi gave them farming and writing (etc.). Lai's version queers this origin story of human beings. Nu Wa takes on human form because of her desire for another woman. When humans engage in sex for pleasure, the creator god Nu Wa averts her eyes so they will not be self-conscious. Nu Wa then gives sex a secondary function—reproduction. In other words, the reproduction function is secondary to the pleasure function. In one short chapter, then, Lai rewrites the Chinese creation myth, the Christian creation myth, and "The Little Mermaid," offering the validation of a queer desire and practice in the foundational myths of the culture.

Nu Wa later meets and falls in love with the titular character, Salt Fish Girl. When the patriarch attempts to separate them, they leave for the city, where both predatory men and colonizing white women also undermine their relationship.

The other storyline features Miranda, a young woman who is born with a strong bodily odor, described as a combination of "cat piss" and "pepper." Nothing she and her parents do can make the smell go away; it is encoded in her physical and cultural DNA. She lives in a future, semi-dystopian British Columbia, where people live in company-branded enclaves. As she breaks away from her parents, and as she learns of the inequities in her world, she meets Evie, a fugitive clone who is 0.3% carp—and therefore legally nonhuman. The two reproduce in a final scene that brings the novel full circle, invoking the creation of humans by Nu Wa in the first chapter. (I will tell you that Miranda and Evie mirror Nu Wa and Salt Fish Girl, but I won't say how.)

Salt Fish Girl offers a compelling critique of Western capitalism. In the Nu Wa chapters, we see NW and SFG's vulnerability in the city. They resort to pickpocketing in order to survive, until a factory blackmails SFG into working there. The work is steady and, though dehumanizing, puts food on their table. In the Miranda chapters, however, Lai really makes the case. Every enclave is controlled by a corporation. Miranda's father is a virtual "tax collector" for a corporation. Once he has collected the taxes, the corporation then beats the money out of him. In other words, the ruling class enact violence upon every citizen, even those who work for them. These corporations also control all goods and services inside the enclaves. Miranda discovers that Dr. Flowers has been manufacturing clones to exploit in the factories. The clones were all derived from a Chinese woman who had been interned in a work camp after

World War II. Her body, however, was used as the source of all the clones (another queer reproduction). Evie and other escaped clones work their "economic sabotage" on the factories. More importantly, they have devised a way to reproduce and live outside the capital system. This, the corporations cannot allow. In the end, Miranda and Evie find a space outside the system, as well.

Salt Fish Girl also illustrates some of the ways in which Western colonialism has damaged individuals and cultures. As Nu Wa and Salt Fish Girl struggle in the city, Edwina, a white woman all dressed in white, approaches Nu Wa and takes her away. She takes Nu Wa to the Island of Mist and Forgetfulness. Edwina uses Nu Wa for her own purposes and then abandons her, leaving her to pay (literally and figuratively) the consequences. Worse, Nu Wa forgets her native tongue, the fate of many immigrants and exiles. When she returns to Salt Fish Girl and to her village, she can no longer communicate with them. The loss and separation are painful and drive Nu Wa to take drastic measures.

In the end, *Salt Fish Girl* decenters the heterosexual relationship and heterosexual reproduction. All the conceptions here take place mythologically or technologically. The novel also decenters heterosexual characters, with all four primary characters being queer women. Furthermore, the novel decenters Western narratives (even as it draws on, incorporates, and modifies) some of them. The events of the novel are focalized through a Chinese perspective. Similarly, it decenters Western science. Certainly, elements of Western science are here, especially in the technologies in the enclaves and the cloning techniques of Dr. Flowers. But *Salt Fish Girl* represents the Western technologies as harmful, dangerous, *as implicated in the very social and political problems of the world.* Finally, in one of the most telling recenterings, the novel favors a cyclical model of time over the Western linear model. While each of the two sections of the novel progress linearly (and are time stamped at the beginning of each chapter), the two storylines represent a cyclical repetition of identities and events. The novel ends, "Everything will be alright, I thought, until next time" (269).

That Larissa Lai knows the history of science fiction I have no doubt. She draws from and intertwines bits and pieces from myths and religion (often fodder for SF), from folk tales, and from SF texts such as *Frankenstein* and *Blade Runner*. That Lai also understands the colonial and Western biases in much SF I also have no doubt. Lai wants to take the traditions and tropes of SF and accomplish something else. She wants to queer our expectations of the genre. She wants to offer representations of queer lives. And she wants to articulate a queer space, a "queer futurity" (see the work of Wendy Pearson for more on this) in which community, family, and reproduction are all reimagined.

17. What's YOUR Superpower?

I'm an optimist who believes that whatever happens next has got to be better than what we already have
—Su J. Sokol, "Je me souviens"

ON SEVERAL OCCASIONS, I have had a discussion with my grandchildren about superheroes, and particularly, about superhero films. They really enjoy superhero movies. They ask me what my favorite superhero is. I respond by saying, "I don't really have a superhero." "What do you mean you don't have a superhero? How is that possible?" I then explain that the premise seems to be that we wait for a superhero, for someone with some otherworldly power, to come along and rescue us all. They stop an alien invasion; they stop a steaming locomotive; they put the bad guys in jail. (Before I get a ton of objections, I do understand that that is a gross over-generalization, but I was trying to make a larger point with them.) I say, "I don't like the idea that you will wait for someone else to save us. I think that YOU can be that superhero. You can be the change you want to see happen in this world."

Which brings me to "Je me souviens" [I Remember] by Su J. Sokol (xe/xyr). The story first appeared in 2012 in *The Future Fire*, edited by Djibril al-Ayad (he/him), and was reprinted in 2016 in *Glittership Year One*, edited by Keffy R. M. Kehrli (he/him). Sokol, as far as I can tell, has published two SF stories and one SF novel. On xyr homepage, xe describes xerself as a "social rights activist" and "writer of speculative, liminal, and

103

interstitial fiction." Though hailing from Brooklyn, NY, Sokol has relocated to Montréal, QC.

"Je me souviens" is a beautiful short story that takes on, in a very short space, social activism, protest, student rights, imprisonment and torture of dissidents, sexual identity, queer families, and social and personal responsibilities.

Gabriel was abducted by the authorities, imprisoned, and tortured in his home country (presumably somewhere in Latin America). Why? Maybe because of his political activities. Maybe because of who his parents were. Maybe because he's queer. He doesn't really even know. But he's now found his way to Canada, in part because of the help of Arielle. After his arrival, Gabriel and Arielle have married, a political marriage. They have a child, Raphaël. Gabriel has become a citizen and a teacher.

Gabriel is convinced that Arielle has superpowers and that Raphaël will have superpowers. He tells him so. He also believes that he has powers himself. Equally as important, he believes in villains and super villains. He senses their evil. He cannot back away from them.

The students in Québec have gone on strike, and Gabriel is a political creature. He feels sympathy for his students; he wants to be on the picket lines with them. Gabriel and his friend Luc mobilize the teachers to participate, to protect their students from the police in riot gear. After that, he feels "invincible." At a larger demonstration the following night, Gabriel feels emboldened, but also feels drawn to the "evil" men dressed in black. He's found a calling.

Another night, Gabriel takes out his superhero costume, the one from the old country, the one his mother had sewn for him. And he heads to another demonstration. Pictures of him dressed in his costume take over social media. He goes viral. He faces consequences from school, from the government. But as demonstrations intensify, as police response increases, he cannot stay home; he cannot not go. As he is knocked over and knocked out, he *remembers*. "Je me souviens." He remembers the old demonstration in his home country, remembers the police taking them away, remembers that it was *his* fault. But as he is being beaten to death down below, little Raphaël has seen his father from the balcony above. Rapha jumps. Rapha flies.

His father had always told him that he had superpowers. Gabriel always told Rapha that one day he would be able to fly. And now he has jumped from a balcony to save his father. And, he does. He saves his father. He landed on the policeman's back, he whispered in his ear the magic words, "Je me souviens."

Gabriel has lived through and has survived unspeakable horrors. And, yet, he cannot turn away from the evil of an oppressive state; he cannot turn his back on a student who is abused at home; he cannot turn his back on the students' cause. His parents were academics and did not believe in superheroes, yet his mother sewed him a costume. His parents did not believe in superheroes, and, yet, Gabriel seeks out evil and stops it.

Gabriel believes in superheroes and convinces his son that he is one. And his son, with nothing more than his homemade cape, leaps into action. When he whispers into the policeman's ears, he is reclaiming and redefining the words of his father. When Gabriel says "I remember," he means his guilt and his suffering. When Raphaël says, "I remember," he is telling the officer that he will not forget. And he will not go away.

This is the superhero story that I want my grandchildren to read. Gabriel does not have super strength or super speed or super intelligence. He has super humanity. Super empathy. Gabriel does not wait for someone else—someone less *vulnerable* in every sense of that word—to stand up for his students; he does so himself. And Gabriel has imparted this to his son, who, like his father, leaps into action when needed.

In this short story, Sokol offers a queer family, a woman, and a gay man who have married for political reasons and the desire for a child. Further, xe offers a queering of the superhero tale. Gabriel has a provocative origin story, but he is not a mutant. He is a loving husband, father, teacher, and friend.

He is a superhero I can believe in.

18. Queer Love in the Time of Pandemic

I HAVE LONG argued that science fiction is not in the future prediction business. Oh, I know, sometimes someone gets it right. Readers gleefully comb through *Brave New World* and catalog the number of things Huxley got right. Less frequently, they catalog what he got wrong. Viewers happily point to reality mirroring fiction in the Star Trek universe, for example, the development of a tricorder. But it also gets a LOT wrong.

Sometimes, though, you read a text and think, that's a little too close to home. In "Imago," by Tristan Alice Nieto (she/her), the author offers a protagonist who experienced a pandemic and now inhabits a post-pandemic world. Reading "Imago" in 2020-21 is a little unsettling. Even so, it is also quite beautiful.

I know next to nothing about Nieto. Her online presence is minimal. Apparently by design, for the author's home page lacks the usual Bio or About page. Nieto worked in the film industry for a few years, including working as the "stereoscopic compositor" on *World War Z*, *Gravity*, *Guardians of the Galaxy*, and *Pixels*. She notes that *Gravity* was a highlight, *Pixels* a lowlight. Since 2015, she has worked more on small budget, independent films, and written a few stories. She wrote and directed the short film *Autoportrait* (2021), in which a transgender woman struggles with feelings of entrapment during the pandemic lockdown.

The story "Imago" appeared in 2017 in the collection *Meanwhile, Elsewhere: Science Fiction and Fantasy from Transgender Writers*. It was reprinted in May 2021, in *Far Out: An*

Anthology of Recent Queer Science Fiction and Fantasy (ed. Paula Guran, Night Shade).

In the story, Tabitha is an entomologist, specializing in lepidoptery (butterflies). She awakens in the morgue. She has been brutally murdered and her eyes stolen. In this future world, however, scientists have developed Revivranol, a drug that returns the dead to life. The down side is that the second life is temporary, lasting only for a few days. The other downside is that memory is frequently "fractured," or splintered, leaving the newly undead searching for answers and information. Tabitha awakens with the image of someone lying next to her. And much of the story is Tabitha's migration back to "her."

Earlier in her life, Tabitha was a survivor of the pandemic, the White Death. When she was young, the White Death was pervasive: every week, someone she knew got sick and died. "You got sick, you turned white, you became agitated, then paranoid, then psychotic, and then you died" (353). She turned white, but did not die. She became "the albino kid," a pariah. Everyone feared that she was a vector. Understandably, that affected her whole life. The pathogen was finally identified, and death rates declined. But that did not change much for Tabitha.

She did, however, possess some rather amazing mechanical eyeballs—compound butterfly eyes. They increased her color vision; they tracked in 3D telemetry; they recorded and stored data; they superimposed Augmented Reality atop everything she saw. And they were ripped out of her head and stolen. Stolen by a man who was told by the Red Witch that she could cure him of the White Death if he brought her Tabitha's eyes.

As part of her research as an entomologist, she had built a set of "tiny robot butterflies." They were meant to fly alongside migrating butterflies and track data. With her eyeballs gone, she connects these tiny drones to her visual network and sees through all of them as they hover and fly. The experience is overwhelming. In the end, though, they lead her back to her old eyes, to the person who has them, to the reason she was killed, and most importantly, to the person she has lost. Tabitha finds her way back to "her," to Deanne.

By the end of the story, Nieto makes the title reference clear. In five places throughout the story, Nieto provides information about butterflies: about "retaining learned behaviors," about eyes, about migration patterns, about persistence, about life spans. The final notes remind us that the "imago" or "adult stage" of the Spring Azure butterfly lives only a few days. Much like our resurrected narrator.

However, while entomologists use *imago* to refer to the adult form of an insect that has gone through metamorphosis, psychologists also use the term to describe the idealized mental image of someone who influences behavior. In many instances, that person is a parent or parent-figure. Here, though, that figure is Deanne. Her. The love of Tabitha's life. The reason why she makes the harrowing migration back to Deanne's grave.

Apart from the cool technology, apart from the amazing vision of butterflies and Tabitha, it is the drive, the compulsion to migrate "home" that centers this story. Tabitha retains memory of Deanne through her metamorphosis; Tabitha makes use of her very short second life to migrate back to that which she loves. She has recovered her memories of Deanne; she remembers Deanne's acceptance of her as a trans woman (another metamorphosis); and Deanne has taught Tabitha to recognize her own beauty. And, by extension, her own humanity.

"Imago" is horrifying. It is heart-wrenching. And it is beautiful. Nieto taps into our fear of contagion, our fear of change, and our fear of Otherness. As a survivor of the pandemic, as a trans woman, Tabitha has always been Other. Tabitha carries with her, and on her, the scars (literal and metaphorical) of the pandemic. Nieto intertwines Tabitha's transformations with those of butterflies. The beautiful, ephemeral life of the butterfly is the life of Tabitha. Metamorphosis from caterpillar to imago is impossibly amazing and beautiful. Tabitha's love of Deanne compels her forward. That love and acceptance gives her first and second lives beauty and meaning. That love allows Tabitha to understand and accept her own beauty and her own significance.

A great gift, indeed, especially in the midst of a pandemic....

19. Love and Sex at the End of the Earth

> *You can't make anything any better....*
> *The world is what it is. Unless you destroy it*
> *and start all over again, there's no changing it.*
> —N. K. Jemisin, *The Fifth Season*

IT WOULD SEEM that little can be said about N. K. Jemisin's Broken Earth (2015-2017) series that has not already been said. The number of awards that these three books have won would fill the rest of this essay. Jemisin (she/her) was the first writer to win the "Best Novel" Hugo Award in three consecutive years. That fact bears some reflection. It is a staggering accomplishment. And I have thoughts on *why* it was so successful. I'll come back to that.

The Fifth Season (I'll only talk about the first book in the series) features a far-future Earth, devastated by climate change. The entire planet seems hell-bent on expelling humans from it. Over time, certain people have developed the ability to communicate with and control elements of the Earth: they quell earthquakes; they move rocks and soil. They are called "orogenes," and they are feared, hated, and killed. They are legally non-humans. The novel follows one orogene though childhood, training, motherhood, and heartbreak. Our protagonist is Damaya when she is young, Syenite once she passes her training, and Essun when she has turned her back on it all.

Many critics and reviewers have written about the environmental issues in the novel. The Earth is angry, and the human inhabitants struggle. Over and over the Earth wipes out human achievements, and humans start over again. The histories (stonelore) help preserve our collective memory against the ravages of Father Earth. Most people live quite close to the land, with very little excess. Although not explicitly clear in this volume, the suggestion is that the we are the vectors, we have precipitated this devastation. Fiction for the post-Anthropocene.

Many critics and reviewers have written about the racial politics of the novels. The parallels to the slavery system in the United States are unmistakable. The Guardians control and punish the orogenes as slaveholders did their slaves. Furthermore, Jemisin points out that the orogenes have built the entire system; the Stillness, the Fulcrum, *all of it* was built on the backs of the enslaved orogenes. And, yet, they are devalued and dehumanized. Inasmuch as the novel appeared in 2015, the parallels to the present-day treatment of BIPOC in the United States are clear. The Guardians can "stop-and-frisk" them for any (or no) reason. The orogenes can be lynched and hunted down without repercussions.

For this essay, though, I would like to focus on love and sex. In several moments, in several characters, Jemisin explores sexuality in the Stillness. At the Fulcrum, Damaya meets Binhof, a precocious child who has been born into a family of privilege and power. She is expected to take on a leadership role, but she rejects this role. For Binhof is trans, and the leadership has no place for a girl/woman—except for breeding—and Binhof wants no part of that. In the circles of power, sex and sexuality play familiar roles. Men have positions of power, women do not. Transwomen have no place and leave the community altogether.

We also learn that although Alabaster has sex with women because the Fulcrum requires him to. His desire is for men. When young, he had a male lover, another advanced orogene. One day, as they were looking for a place to be alone and intimate, a Guardian attacked and killed his lover. The Guardian directed his lover's orogeny inward, and his lover exploded. The Guardian grinned as he killed him. Did the Guardian hate orogenes? Did he hate homosexuality? Did he hate Alabaster? "All Guardians are killers," says Alabaster (288). But the message to Alabaster, of course, was to guard against the Guardians. To police himself, as always happens with the marginalized.

After another nearly fatal encounter with a Guardian in the community of Allia, a Stone Eater takes Alabaster and Syenite to an island off the coast, Meov. Here, love and sex are given freedom of expression. Alabaster quickly enters into a romantic/sexual relationship with Innon, the political leader of Meov and captain of its ship. At times, Syenite is included in the relationship, in the lovemaking, but cannot define it. She doesn't have the terms: "And what do they even call this? It's not a threesome, or a love triangle. It's a two-and-a-half-some, an affection dihedron. (And, well, maybe it's love)" (372).

In the confines of the Stillness, under the sway of the Fulcrum and the Guardians, sex, gender, and sexuality are all conscribed and coerced. Girls, transkids, and queer folx are all marginalized, shunned, and murdered. On the island off the coast, they have no such strictures. Alabaster, Innon, and Syenite are free to have whatever relationship they want, even if they can't quite name it. The other islanders merely laugh and joke that Syenite gets to sleep with two of the handsomest men on the island.

And, yet, though I have tried to pull out the moments regarding sex and love, they cannot really be separated. The attitudes about sex and sexuality are part and parcel of the land, of the politics. Syenite the slave has little control over her sexuality, over her body, over her reproduction. She must reproduce for the Fulcrum or expect consequences. She must reproduce with Alabaster, the talented orogene. Only on Meov, where the orogenes are in charge, can that be different.

In *The Fifth Season*, Jemisin represents what philosophers, political activists, feminists, and queer activists have long been saying: give the underrepresented a voice; start with the marginalized to build a more equitable society. As disability activists have shown, if we begin from the place of access, then we construct a society (and a city) that works for every member. Jemisin shows what happens when we begin with the orogenes and construct a society in which they are in charge. Meov is not a paradise, and it is not a perfect society. It is no utopia. The residents of Meov cannot fully sustain their way of life on the island without provisions from outside. Nevertheless, it is a society in which neither orogenes nor stills (those who do not have the ability) are marginalized or killed. It is a society in which Alabaster can freely express his love and desire for Innon. When representatives of the Fulcrum reappear, then it all crumbles.

In the end, the novel offers an intersectional critique of systems of power. Each element of the system is implicated in another, depends on another. The domestication of the orogenes relies on a racist system that marginalizes them and renders them vulnerable, and compulsory heterosexuality is necessary for perpetuating the families and systems of power. The answer, then, would be to address all the issues together—what philosopher Marilyn Frye (she/her) has called a macroscopic approach instead of a microscopic approach.

As I noted above, the Broken Earth series first appeared in 2015, just prior to the election of Donald Trump. It appeared in the midst of a social and political reckoning regarding racial killing of people of color. It appeared in the midst of a social and political reevaluation of trans rights. And Jemisin's novels, with their intersectional approach to race, ethnicity, sexuality, and environment, were exactly what people wanted to read.

This approach is exactly why she was the first author to win three consecutive Hugo Awards. Nora Jemisin tapped into the social and political Zeitgeist and produced The Broken Earth series at exactly the moment it was needed most.

20. "Bloodchild" and the Queer Family

IN 1993 MARK DERY (he/him) coined the term Afrofuturism, and it has been in circulation ever since (Dery). The early definitions and examinations of Afrofuturism saw it in art, music, and literature, drawing on a wide range of forms and genres and expanding the Western understanding of the world to include non-Western perspectives. The painter Jean-Michel Basquiat (he/him), the musicians Sun Ra (he/him) and George Clinton (he/him), and writers Samuel R. Delany and Octavia E. Butler (she/her) were all included as exemplars of art that addressed African American themes and concerns in the context of 20th-century technoculture. The term gave a name and place to an amorphous set of works and artists, provided a category for analysis, for marketing, and for conversation. With the exception of Butler, the list was male. The term, the list of people associated with it, and the works themselves have all shifted over time. The newer versions, the newer practitioners of Afrofuturism include Janelle Monáe, N. K. Jemisin, Nnedi Okorafor, among others.

In the previous Shade, I wrote about Jemisin's *The Fifth Season* and its intersectional take on contemporary politics. A comparison of Butler's "Bloodchild" and Jemisin's *The Fifth Season* illustrates the difference between earlier versions of Afrofuturism and newer articulations of it. In her discussion of "Bloodchild," Butler avoids the political interpretation; Jemisin demands it.

In June 1984, Butler published "Bloodchild" in *Isaac Asimov's Science Fiction Magazine*. In 1985, it won the Hugo,

Nebula, *Locus*, and *SF Chronicle* awards for best novelette: a remarkable feat.

"Bloodchild" tells a story of one family of humans on an alien planet. This planet is inhabited by the T'lic, a reptilian-like race, with scaly skin, multiple legs, and an ovipositor. Following a period of armed conflict (during which, we can infer, humans attempted to colonize the planet), the T'lic keep all humans confined to a fenced-in space, and they use the humans for reproductive purposes. Although the T'lic used to deposit their young in indigenous animals, they have discovered that humans make better hosts and produce stronger children. Furthermore, unfertilized T'lic eggs (a) get humans high and (b) extend their lives. So, in order to curry favor, the T'lic selectively dole out eggs to humans. In the story, the T'lic T'Gatoi has come to the home of Gan. T'Gatoi has known Gan since he was born, and she always intended to impregnate him. However, when Gan witnesses a birth go horribly wrong (picture the alien bursting forth in the first *Alien* movie), he has second thoughts. T'Gatoi tells him that she had always planned to impregnate him, but that she would impregnate Gan's sister, Xuan Hoa, if necessary. Gan relents.

Many a reader, critic, and student has read this story as an allegory about slavery. The humans are confined on the reserve; they are limited in access to resources; they cannot own guns. Recall that Huey Newton (he/him) said, "An unarmed people are slaves or are subject to slavery at any given moment" (1967). Butler likely knew of Newton's statement. Humans exist solely, it would seem, for the benefit of the T'lic. Just as slaveholders did, the T'lic use humans to increase their own numbers, to insure a steady, readily available supply of breeders. They keep the humans enthralled by suggesting that they are "family," by holding out the promise of life-extending drugs. Gan's older brother, Qui, has seen through the fiction, and he rejects it out of hand. He wants no part of the system. But Gan feels special, feels chosen.

Is that not a description of slavery? One group of people keeps and uses another group of people for their own benefit. Butler, however, rejected that reading of the story. Indeed, in an afterword in her story collection, she noted that people only read "Bloodchild" as being about slavery because she, Octavia Butler, is black. No, she said, "Bloodchild" is a "love story."

So, "Bloodchild" may or may not be about slavery, but is it a queer SF story? Formally, I don't think that Butler queers readers' expectations of the genre. SF readers have all seen alien contact stories before; they have all seen human-alien relationships before; they have all seen colonial stories before. By and large, though, humans tend to prevail, and here Gan capitulates. Furthermore, "Bloodchild" is probably not the first male pregnancy story they have read. So what makes it queer?

Reproduction. Desire. Love.

For one, the human-alien system of reproduction is queer. A large alien reptile deposits larvae inside a human male. Yes, the T'lic use it as a means of reproducing their own futurity. Not only will they have more babies, but better and healthier babies! Gan and the humans are also perpetuated. Yes, an occasional human perishes during "birth"; however, the T'lic impregnate males in order to keep human females for human reproduction. From this logic, then, the reproductive process seems no different than the logic of hetero repro. And, yet, the system produces a radically different family structure. It does not replicate the nuclear family. While we know little of the T'lic home life, we do see the T'lic inserted into the human nuclear family, creating different filiations, different allegiances. And, in the end, is Gan's connection to his Xuan Hoa, or to T'Gatoi? Is it about human futurity or T'lic futurity?

What is the basis for Gan's desire for reproducing with T'Gatoi? Why does he want to participate in the very system that constrains him, marginalizes him, exploits him? T'Gatoi has been a part of the family for all of Gan's life. Her appearance, her presence, her assumptions seem entirely familiar to Gan. He has grown up with the expectation that he would host children for T'Gatoi. He has been socialized to accept this situation. In some ways, then, his biology is his destiny, but even here, it's Gan and not Qui. When T'Gatoi wraps her rows of "arms" around him, readers often squirm. But not Gan. It feels like home.

Still Butler asks us to think about "Bloodchild" as a love story. When T'Gatoi says it's time for him to be impregnated, Gan balks. Certainly, the image of the larvae eating their way out of Bran Lomas gives him pause. Even so, Gan wants something more from T'Gatoi. He wants T'Gatoi to say that it means something to her. She cannot give him this reassurance. She says she will use Xuan Hoa, instead. When Gan says, "No, use me," is it because of his love for T'Gatoi? Because of a desire to feel special and chosen? Because of his love for Xuan Hoa? Is he saving *her* from the horror of Bran Lomas?

Has Gan come to love his enslaver? With the power inequality in this relationship, it cannot be love—not as we understand it here and now. I would not want to say that the story is queer because the alien enslaves and exploits Gan. I would not say that it is queer because Gan reproduces T'lic futurity. Instead, I would suggest that "Bloodchild" is queer because it challenges us to think about familial and reproductive norms. It asks us to think about relationships, about family, about reproduction, and about love.

21. Aliens and Drag Queens in "The Moon Room"

IMAGINE THAT YOU'RE in a dimly-lit room, maybe a bar, and you see someone out of the corner of your eye. Just a flash. In that flash, you're not quite sure what it is you've seen. The person seems to change shape, change colors. Is it an effect of the lighting? Is it an afterimage? Is it the onset of palinopsia? Is it a shapeshifter? An alien? In Maria Romasco Moore's "The Moon Room," the answer is aliens. Isn't the answer always "aliens"?

Romasco Moore (she/her), from Baton Rouge, has published only a few SF stories. She published five stories between 2012 and 2020, and a collection, *Ghostographs*, in 2018. "The Moon Room" appeared in the webmagazine, *Kaleidotrope* (2020).

In the story, Sasha works a day job in a café and takes pictures at night of patrons and drag queens in a bar called The Moon Room. But Sasha has a complicated history. Her mother says they came to the United States when Sasha was five, but Sasha can find no record of the town they came from. Her mother says that they came from Russia, but her mother's accent does not sound like other Russian accents. Her mother will provide no further details of Sasha's childhood. Furthermore, Sasha has trouble staying in shape.

Samuel Delany has written about moments like this. He writes about how language functions differently in SF. In one of the examples he provides, he writes the sentence: "He turned on his left side" (1987, 139). A reader not thinking she was reading science fiction might interpret that to mean that the character was sleeping and adjusted himself into a more comfortable position. A reader thinking they were reading SF might take that to mean that the character is a robot, a cyborg, or a technologically-enhanced being who has flipped a switch and activated his left side.

In this story, "Sasha has trouble staying in shape." A non-SF reader might think that Sasha wishes that she weighed less and that she has trouble with diet or exercise. An SF reader might understand that Sasha's body literally changes shape. The power of SF language offers another (or different) layer of meaning. Sasha has a hard time controlling her shape, and it is *painful* to do so. So she drinks alcohol—a lot of it—because it helps with the pain of staying in shape. The alcohol helps Sasha cope with the pain of being in the wrong body shape. That sort of self-medication is often reported by trans individuals who speak of the pain of being in the wrong body.

So, when Sasha sees a glimpse of a man in the bar who seems to shift shape, if ever so briefly, if only in a momentary glimpse, she has to find him. The first time she finds him, she's too drunk to remember anything. She remembers nothing of the conversation, but she does have one telling photograph from that encounter. The second time she meets him, she is sober and she has a picture of him, not "in shape." She has found one of her kind: "Most Fortunate."

Much of the story takes places in The Moon Room, with appearances by Bambi Deerest and Moonmama. Sasha lives with Bradley, who also "transforms" before he performs at The Moon Room. When Bradley suggests that she drinks too much, Sasha calls him sexist. Bradley begins to say "You're not really a woman," though he catches himself and does not finish the thought. Is Bradley's un-uttered thought merely a reflection of what people say to trans individuals all the time? In a non-SF story, yes. In an SF story, not *only* that.

Most Fortunate's advice to Sasha is to forget everything he told her, to force herself in to the "right shape," and to live her life as she has been. But Sasha cannot do it any longer. She cannot remain in the wrong shape. She cannot deny who and what she is.

In the case of Sasha, the metaphor has become literal. She feels as though she is in the wrong shape. It *hurts* to be in the wrong shape. And the only answer for her is to cast off the words of her mother, Most Fortunate, and all of society and say, "This is me. This is who I am." She must transform into her own, true self.

And when she does, she "blazes[s] up and out until she fills the room," until she is "bright and large and strange."

As I've noted, Sasha carries a Single Lens Reflex camera and shoots with film. She develops 24 frames a day. She loves the "magic" of watching the image develop over time—as if it transforms into its true shape. In the story, we often see Sasha examining the negatives, in which the colors are all inverted. When she sees her first negative images of Most Fortunate, his irises are brown, his skin is pink, and his blood is red. Romasco Moore leaves it there, without explaining. But when that negative image is developed into a positive print, his irises would be blue; his skin would be green, and his blood would be a lighter green. Before she leaves the bathroom, she absorbs her camera, with all her surfaces acting like film.

After coming out of the bathroom, her most immediate fears are quelled. When Moonmama, the queen whom she photographs almost every night, sees Sasha emerge from the bathroom in her own body, her own shape, Moonmama can only smile.

In this short story, Romasco Moore demonstrates the negative effects of compelling yourself to be something, or someone, you are not. The denial has deleterious effects on Sasha. On anyone. Romasco Moore demonstrates the power of transformation. After Sasha takes on her own body shape, she is an amazing technicolor blaze of color and light. And in order to do so, Romasco Moore demonstrates the power of SF language and the beauty of coming out of the bathroom.

22. Bitch Planet? "You're Already on It"

IN 1977, THE Combahee River Collective, a group of Black feminists, issued a statement, in which they articulate the necessity of an analysis and a politics that includes gender, race, class, *and* sexuality. In part, the group members were responding to some of the analyses of white, second-wave feminists. In part, they were responding to their own everyday lived experiences. In the statement, they discuss the reality of interlocking systems of oppression. A few years later (1989), Kimberlé Crenshaw (she/her) published "Demarginalizing the Intersection of Race and Sex," which picks up the Combahee River Collective's call and formulates the concept/term "intersectionality."

In 2014, long-time comics writer Kelly Sue DeConnick (she/her) began a series of comics called *Bitch Planet*. DeConnick had written for *Spider-Man*, *Castle*, and *Captain Marvel* (Marvel) and *Supergirl*, *Adventures of Superman*, and *Aquaman* (DC), among many others. She also currently writes *Pretty Deadly* (with Emma Ríos) for Image Comics. *Bitch Planet* ran for 10 issues, until 2017. Later that same year, other writers produced five new issues set in the world of *Bitch Planet* (collectively published as Triple Feature). From its inception, *Bitch Planet* sought to offer an intersectional analysis of contemporary gender, racial, class, and sexual politics. The storyline considers interlocking systems of oppression and features a diverse cast of characters.

The intersectional approach in *Bitch Planet* is deliberate. In each of the ten issues, the comic is followed by an editorial by DeConnick, and an essay (and sometimes an interview) on questions of intersectional feminism. The essay in Issue 1 by Danielle Henderson (she/her) addresses resistance to feminism. In Issue 2, Tasha Fierce Tasha Fierce (they/them) addresses cultural misapprehensions of feminism. In Issue 3 Megan Carpentier (she/her) addresses the difficulty and costs of bodily non-compliance. In Issue 4, Mikki Kendall (she/her), citing Crenshaw, offers a reminder that feminism *needs* to be for *all* women. In Issue 5, Lindy West (she/her) confronts the narrative of victimhood, and connection of victimhood and passivity.

The comic narrative itself offers a near future in which patriarchy has been reestablished in full force (think of Gilead in *The Handmaid's Tale*). Here, the system is called the New Protectorate (a lot of work is being done just in that name!). The Fathers rule every element of society, and they demand and compel compliance to the patriarchs. Those women who do not comply are labeled "Non-Compliant" and shipped off Earth to a prison colony called the Auxiliary Compliance Outpost (ACO). Colloquially, the ACO is known as Bitch Planet. Women can be sent there for any number of "reasons": their appearance, queerness, genetic conditions, and, of course, at the whim of a man. Perhaps he has a mistress and would like to get his wife out of the way. Just send her to the ACO.

The New Protectorate broadcasts propaganda via state-owned media. Viewing is mandatory. When Father Josephson learns of viewer response to an athlete who died on screen, he has an epiphany. In the New Protectorate, Duemila ("two thousand") is a popular sport—think of a more violent version of rugby. They will assemble a team of women from the ACO and pit them against a men's team. Their onscreen deaths will be a ratings bonanza! None of it goes quite as planned.

They task Kamu Kogo with putting together and training the women's team. Kamu Kogo is in the ACO, looking for her sister, a trans woman. One of the team members is Penelope

Rolle, who is a big woman. Her size is something that she wears proudly (as a tattoo on her arm). Prior to being sent to the ACO, she owned a bakery called Born Big. She can no longer tolerate the propaganda regarding beauty, appearance, and dieting. Another team member, Meiko Maki, is the daughter of two revolutionary parents, and is "non-compliant" because she killed a man who was threatening her family.

They eventually discover Eleanor Doane, who was once the President, but has been locked away by the New Protectorate for years. You can bet the inmates are going to break Eleanor out.

Since Bitch Planet is a women's prison, DeConnick and team had to address the cultural trope. How many sexploitation films have made use of the women's prison for the male gaze? In *Bitch Planet*, we see the women arrive, stripped, humiliated. We see the women lined up for showers. But textually, the authors attempt to complicate and queer the scene. Unlike the sexploitation films of the 1960s and '70s, the women represent a wide range of races and ethnicities, a wide range of body types. In addition, the women are not presented for a sexual gaze, but rather to create empathy and connection with them.

Nevertheless, DeConnick and crew make use of the male gaze. Behind the showers, a male guard has a small peep hole. So, in this sense, the prisoners *are* subjected to a male gaze. In most sexploitation stories, the male gazing at the naked female prisoner is the viewpoint shared by the reader. In *Bitch Planet*, however, the male gaze gets co-opted. Once they catch the guard, Kam takes advantage of the guard's compromised position and blackmails him onto her team. He becomes an important asset to Kam.

As I have noted before, Queer SF takes many forms, has many goals. For one, DeConnick and team seek to queer the very conventions of SF comics. They look at the form and its history, they look at the conventions, and they shift them. They put women of color and queer women at the center of the story. They emphasize and espouse non-normative ideas. They expose cultural attitudes (about gender, about race, about size, about sexuality) and offer new norms.

In her essay in Issue 1, Danielle Henderson says that we do not really need to imagine some future world in which non-compliant women are shipped off-world. She argues that we already live on Bitch Planet. Through its characters, through its narrative, through the extra-narrative elements of the comics, through the essays and interviews, and through merch, *Bitch Planet* offers a queer take on SF comics and what they can do.

What *we* can do if we're all non-compliant.

23. Karel Čapek, Robots, and Queer Family

You still stand watch, O human star,
burning without a flicker,
perfect flame, bright and resourceful spirit.
—Karel Čapek, *R. U. R.*

IN 1920, THE Czech writer Karel Čapek (he/him) wrote *R.U.R. (Rossum's Universal Robots)*. In the play, he used the Czech word "robota" to describe the beings created to work in the factories. Robota means "worker" or "slave," but has since come to signify an artificial being. The factory creates these robota, which are synthetic beings from organic material. So, they were not metallic or mechanical beings, but made of artificial flesh and blood. These robota also have intelligence and can think for themselves. Although initially content to work in the factories for humans, they eventually rebel and take over.

Arguably, although Franz Kafka's (he/him) 1915 novella, *Metamorphosis* gained greater recognition, *R.U.R.* and *Metamorphosis* both deal with the alienation of modern life and work, and the exploitation of people's labor. In Kafka's story, the alienated Gregor Samsa discovers he has turned into a beetle. In Čapek's play, the alienated robots rebel and take over. Both, in short, address some of the changes wrought by modern, technological society.

In 2011, comic writer Blue Dellaquanti (they/them) began work on their self-published webcomic, *O Human Star*. In the very last page of the comic, Dellaquanti provides the (above) quote from Čapek that serves as the title of Dellaquanti's

129

webcomic. In an interview, Dellaquanti says that the origins for the comic came in a dream. Their dream began with the basic premise of a man who wakes up in a synthetic body, and Dellaquanti developed it from there.

The comic ran from 2012-2020, with weekly updates, sometimes a single page. *OHS* takes on multiple issues, from autonomy for synthetic beings, to "passing" for queer folx, to the exploitation of labor, and others. Read *OHS*, and then read it again. You'll find even more the second time. At its center it is about three individuals: Alistair Sterling, Brendan Pinsky, and Sulla. The comic is drawn in three basic color palettes, each corresponding to a particular timeframe within the comic: blue (2021), orange/pink (2001), and green (2019ish). Al is a robotics genius, laboring away in his small lab. He hires an assistant, Brendan, right out of MIT. They get off to a rocky start. Like the robota in *R.U.R.*, Brendan is not comfortable with his position or the work he is asked to do by Al. Instead of rebellion, though, Brendan humanizes Al, and they become lovers. After Al dies of an autoimmune disorder, the devastated Brendan tries to recreate Al from a memory recording he had made as Al was on his deathbed. The resurrected Al, however, is not fully comfortable in his new life.

In some sense, *OHS* illustrates the differences of coming out and being a queer person in three different historical moments in time. Within the narrative's timeline, Al was born in 1961, and he had a difficult relationship with his father. Because of his past, because of the time in which he grew up, Al cannot be open about his relationship with Brendan, and it is a source of friction. That tension exacerbates Al's autoimmune condition, and it ultimately causes his death. In other words, his reluctance to be open about his relationship with Brendan kills him. Brendan, though, was born in the mid-80s, and so is much more open and comfortable about his sexuality. Friends and colleagues know he is gay, and he wants to be open with is relationship with Al. Brendan cannot understand Al's reluctance. Finally, Sulla was created in 2006, and has an even more fluid notion of gender and sexuality than Brendan does. More importantly, she has the unflinching support of Brendan when she does transition. Each of the three characters reflect some of the cultural and social biases of three historical periods regarding queer folx. Each of the three represents some of the issues for family and community that queer folx confront on a daily basis.

More than being three individuals, they are very much a queer family. When the synthetic Al is delivered to Brendan's front doorstep, Brendan rejects him. But then he relents. Dellaquanti depicts lovely domestic scenes as the three of them sit around the dining room table. As Brendan returns to work, Al and Sulla go into town together. Sulla catches Al up on the changes of the past 16 years; Al boosts Sulla's self-confidence as she sees a group of school kids. By the end of the comic, Sulla calls Brendan and Al her dads.

Their family replicates, in some ways, a nuclear family, but only superficially. Brendan was 25(ish) years younger than Al when Al was alive. Furthermore, Al is now synthetic and Brendan human. Brendan will continue to age as Al remains as he is. How do they even calculate age difference now? They have a child, a synthetic child whom they both love. Though Sulla is the product of Brendan and Al, she has been produced via non-sexual means. Sulla is their child, but she is also the resurrection of Al—even as she is her own self.

One of the central mysteries of *OHS* is who produced the synthetic Al. Was it Brendan? Lucille? Tsade? Near the end, we discover that Al's synth form was commissioned by Sulla. Because she was intended to be a new Al for Brendan, she felt like a failure. As a trans girl, she felt she had failed her parent. So, she brought Al back for Brendan. So, for one, Sulla enacts the guilt many trans kids feel at disappointing their parents. For another, Al, who is her dad, is produced by Sulla. She brought him to life. Sulla is her father's creator. In the second surprise (though Dellaquanti scatters breadcrumbs throughout), in the final pages, we see Al say that he is not "gay" because "I'm not a man." Does Al mean, "I'm not a man because I'm a synth?" Does he mean, "I'm not man because I'm a woman?" Does he mean, "I'm not a man because I'm non-binary?" The answer remains ambiguous. Nevertheless, on the final page, Al enters a tank in the laboratory in order to transform into his true self, the self he could never be in his human body.

In the end, Dellaquanti creates a queer family comic for the modern age, a modern family, if you will. The lines of affiliation are redefined. The relation of parent and offspring is reimagined. The fluidity of family roles are remade.

It is, perhaps, a family of a queer futurity.

24. Queer Family in Ohio

IN OTHER PLACES, I have written a lot about Ohio. Mostly about some messed-up events and legislative matters. This time, however, I'd like to examine a Queer SF story set in northwest Ohio.

According to Brendan Williams-Childs's (he/him) personal webpage, he was born in Wyoming and studies in Kansas. He has said in an interview that he had a grandmother who lived in Ohio. His webpage also notes that he has published ten stories, though only three of those appear on the Internet Science Fiction Database.

His story "Schwaberow, Ohio" appeared in 2017 in the anthology *Meanwhile Elsewhere: Science Fiction and Fantasy from Transgender Writers*, which was a finalist for the Lambda Literary Award in 2017. After the publisher of that anthology went out of business, Williams-Childs made the story available on *Medium.com*.

The short story focuses on Walt, a trans man who lives with autism, who finds himself at the crossroads of political and technological debates about changing people's identities. Although the story is set physically in northwest Ohio, it's really set ideologically in the midst of a national debate and a national election. In this near future, authorities have developed technological interventions into the human body. Haleigh Thompson, the wife of a presidential candidate, has significant technological enhancements. She is derogatorily referred to as a "cyberbabe." Authorities have also developed "neurological behavioral implants." This wire inserted into the head can be used to "treat" juvenile delinquents. It would be used to "treat" autism. And it would also be used to "treat" trans individuals.

Walt's father is vehemently opposed to the wire, to all technological enhancements. He is not interested in using tech to address Walt's autism. Indeed, he went to prison for stabbing someone with a synthetic heart. But when it's discovered that the wire can also be used to stop people "from being trans," he has a change of heart. Had they the money, Aunt Marianne would simply stick a wire into Walt so "they could stop [Walt] from stimming and being trans" (300). Walt says that Aunt Marianne "would turn me back into a girl, maybe even a girl who isn't autistic" (297). Uncle Ray is a bit more sanguine about Walt. He rudely waves his hand in front of Walt's face to make sure that he is paying attention, but has no particular interest in changing Walt.

First, recent studies are showing a higher incidence of autism in gender diverse populations than in non-gender diverse groups. A study in *Research in Autism Spectrum Disorders* suggests that the incidence of autism is as much as 10 times higher in the adolescent gender variant community than it is in the adolescent cisgender community (Murphy, 2020). Similarly, *Spectrum News* reports a 2020 study of adults in the United Kingdom shows that autism is 5 times more likely among members of the gender diverse community (Dattaro). Walt represents this community.

Second, Walt also represents the differential attitudes about individuals with autism and individuals who are trans. Members of the community at large are likely to think that autism is something that cannot be changed, that it is something they were born with. Members of the mainstream society are likely to think that trans is an illness, or a life style, or a choice that someone makes. They are also likely to think it is a sin or is amoral. And, therefore, even someone opposed to technological intervention might be in favor "fixing" a trans kid.

Third, "Schwaberow" comments on the ways in which our behaviors are scripted. Walt frequently displays repetitive behaviors. For example, he reminds himself of the order to put on his shoes. Walt notes that "It takes five tugs on the blue string to roll the shades up" (296). And, "I sit on the ramp and count the eggs. It takes three minutes. There are sixteen" (296). He completes his chores: "Efficient, measured. Robotic" (308). People in Walt's life have argued that he is trans because he learned and emulated his father's behaviors. Walt believes that the wire, the neural reprogramming, is simply "A script to erase a script" (306). For example, after Walt and Ray spring Walt's mom from jail, she says, "You'll always be my baby" (306). A line she has repeated his whole life. A script that mom reels off whenever she sees Walt. The story suggests that we *all* operate by scripts. That's the process of socialization. The wire would only instill a different set of scripts.

Fourth, Williams-Childs also demonstrates the structural inequalities that trans individuals and individuals with autism face. Ray and Marianne do not have the money or the insurance to pay for the neuropsych intervention. Walt reminds us that a life on medication for a trans person would be expensive—particularly for the state. If the state can use neurological behavioral modification implants, then it can save money in the long term. He also notes that insurance does not cover transition surgery, but it *does* cover "gender dysphoria alleviation" (309). They will pay to try to make someone cis.

Finally, the story demonstrates the importance of online community, even as it shows the ephemerality of it. He is good friends with Rebecca from the "Chicago part of the internet" (296). They are no longer friends with Diana from the "Milwaukee part of the internet" (296). Rebecca is part of the anti-robot-modifications part of the internet, too. Neither of them are OK with the modifications. Apart from community and support, they hang out in subreddits for robo-mods and DIY-trans issues. Sometimes, fam is made.

And so, on Election Day, Walt packs his things and leaves Schwaberow. The only Schwaberow that I know is the Schwaberow Cemetery outside Anna, Ohio. He packs "four sweaters, six shirts, three pairs of pants, an extra pair of shoes. Five hundred and twelve dollars" (309). He leaves the cemetery and heads for Chicago, for his online fam who has supported him.

He heads toward the online fam that does not want to modify him.

25. Trans Time Travel

> *Time travel fictions present special problems because they play with foundational things like time, causation, and the personal identity and free will of the time traveler— and it is not at all clear what any of these things are like in the real world.*
> —John Bigelow, "Time Travel Fiction"
>
> *The future feels lighter than the past. I think I know why you chose it over me, Mama.*
> —Nino Cipri, "The Sound of My Name"

WHO AMONG US has not wanted to take a trip in time? Who has not wanted the opportunity to go back and have another chance? To fix a personal mistake? Who has not wanted to leap ahead and take a glimpse at the world to come, to see what we might otherwise miss? But traveling back in time so often creates these classic paradoxes, such as traveling back in time and having sex with a direct relative, which starts one's own lineage. In such a story (genetics aside), the notion of time seems fixed, since the events of time are in a closed loop. Or, in another kind of story, traveling back in time and altering one tiny fact, the time traveler returns "home" and finds everything changed, or else winks out of existence altogether. In such a story, the notion of time is malleable, but the effects of this are unknown. Or, in a third kind of story, traveling ahead in time and bringing back future knowledge, the traveler thereby alters the future just visited.

Apart from the mechanics of time travel fiction (cf. David Wittenberg, John Bigelow, or David Lewis), what is the thematic desire? What does the author accomplish narratively by using the time travel trope? What does an author of Queer SF hope to accomplish? Nino Cipri (they/them) might offer us some thoughts.

Cipri has been busy. Just look at their Twitter feed. Apart from tweeting, Cipri has published 23 short stories since 2012, three chapbooks, one collection of stories, and two novels. Their story "The Shape of My Name" first appeared on Tor.com. The story has been reprinted four times, including in *Transcendent* (ed., K. M. Szpara, 2015), and it was a finalist for the James Tiptree (now Otherwise) Award. Cipri has also noted in several interviews that they like to play with form. For example, Cipri writes one story in the form of a magazine poll ("Which Super Little Dead Girl™ Are You?" [2017]). In an interview in *Nightmare Magazine,* Cipri says they have also written stories "told as audio transcripts, Wikipedia articles, and editorial notes" (McNeil). "The Shape of My Name" is told in the form of a letter from a child to their mother.

"The Shape of My Name" tells the story of a family that travels in time. The time machine (anachronopede) was built in 1905 and works only for members of the Stone family. The machine recognizes the family DNA. It resides in an underground bunker in the backyard of a house held by the same family for centuries. Time travel is limited to the span between 1905 and August 3, 2321. No one knows what happens on that date and why time travel cannot go past it, probably not something good.... Uncle Dante keeps a hefty book in which he tracks family members during those 306 years, including details of all the family's members, past and future, *except* for our protagonist, whose name and sex are both left blank.

The child's mother comes from a future moment in time. But she knows who she will marry and when. And so she is an "exile" in time in 1947 when Miriam Stone marries Tom Guthrie. Their child is born in 1950. But because the child had no name in the official family history, no one expected the child to live. No one had a name ready.

In some ways, Miriam's plight parallels that of many a 1950s housewife. She felt exiled and trapped there. She stayed at home and took care of the house while Tom was away at work. She did not time travel during pregnancy or after the baby was born. The feminine mystique has her feeling inadequate and alone. Desperate, she takes the child on a time trip at age twelve.

Miriam does have company, though. Dara often stays at the house while Tom is at work (he works two weeks stretches in an oil field). Dara, too, is from the family, from some future moment in time. Miriam and Dara are lovers.

In 1963 (the year *The Feminine Mystique* was published), when the child is not yet thirteen, mom makes that first time trip to see Dara—but a Dara who has not yet met the child. They stay in Dara's house in 1981 for a while, and the child is amazed by all the future technology. Miriam was looking for a way out of the feminine mystique.

The day after they return to 1963, Miriam Guthrie (Stone) packs her bag, leaves a brief note, and leaves her family. She travels as far into the future as she possibly can, beyond the reach of time travel and time travelers. In some ways, Miriam Guthrie (Stone) is a postmodern Nora. When Nora slams closed the front door of the *Doll House*, where does she go? What does she do? Has she *really* escaped the patriarchy that kept her trapped like a plaything? Here, Miriam walks out the front door, with no slamming. She didn't want to wake anyone. And she heads to the end of time. Maybe she's found a way out of the doll house.

When mom bails, Dara is there for the child. Mom had resisted the idea that her child could be trans. Mom insisted on the name she had given the child at birth. Mom bristled when Dara visited and "indulged" the child with name games. And when Miriam can no longer deny her son, she escapes. Leaves him behind. In 2076 Dara helps the child with surgery and recuperation. Dara the queer mom with her queer kid in queer time.

Just prior to having surgery, the child returns to 1954, to see mom, to see if forgiveness was possible. Mother cannot recognize the child as her son.

So, what does Nino Cipri have to tell us about time travel tales? Bigelow suggests that we don't necessarily know what time, and identity, and (I'll extend it to include) family are like in the "real world." "The Shape of My Name" (drawn from Audre Lorde's poem "Artisan") similarly suggests that time is just as malleable and fluid as identity. The story suggests that each of us may be a different person, with a different name, from one day to the next, from one decade to the next. The protagonist notes that the future is free of the weight of the past and so offers the possibility of change.

Of being who you're meant to be.

26. The Heat Death of the Individual

IN 1967, PAMELA ZOLINE (she/her) published a short story in *New Worlds* entitled "The Heat Death of the Universe." The story caused a bit of a furor because it wasn't like anything SF readers had read before. Why was this being published in a science fiction magazine? What were Zoline and editor Michael Moorcock (he/him) doing? The story relates the events of one day in the life of Sarah Boyle, a housewife who is planning a birthday party. She feels as though her own identity has been subsumed into her functions as housewife, mother, and consumer, and as though everything around is winding down into a heat death. In order to maintain some semblance of order, she labels things in her household. It is not a battle that she can win.

In 2016, writer/activist M. Téllez (they/them) published a short story entitled "Heat Death of Human Arrogance." It doubtless owes something to Zoline, and, yet, is wholly its own story with its own aims. Téllez's story first appeared in *Meanwhile, Elsewhere*. That publisher has since gone out of business. A revised version of the story appeared on Téllez's personal blog, *Cyborg Memoirs*. In 2018, it was reprinted in *Transcendent 3* (ed., Bogi Takács [e/em/eir]).

The story centers on two entities (I cannot say "individuals" for reasons that will become apparent). Loma is a "human-identified Earth organism" (255), and Inri is a "third generation Slow Stepper™" (254). Loma is a human, who lives on Earth. She lives in a commune, lives in close proximity to plants, rejects "colonialist expansion into space" (255) and fights for "individual freedoms" (254) for the Slow Steppers™.

Inri, on the other hand, is part of a rhizomatic collective. This particular version of Slow Steppers™ is bipedal and makes regular trips to Mars. The Slow Steppers™ form a "symbiotic relationship" with the bacteria on Mars, in order to cultivate it and bring it into an active state. They are terraforming Mars for human colonization. The Slow Steppers™ are not individuals; they do not think of themselves as individuals. They did not ask Loma or the humans to secure "individual freedoms" for them.

But Loma and Inri have a relationship. Loma uses verbal language for communication; Inri does not. Loma has sexual organs; Inri does not. Inri wears a prosthetic. They cannot quite agree on what "love" is, but they enjoy sensual and sexual pleasures.

Because of what Inri *thinks* Loma means by "love," Inri is quite confused when Loma claims that she would rather die than be shipped off to Mars. When Inri returns from the latest trip to Mars, they are unsure whether Loma has been shipped off, or whether Loma has killed herself. As Inri returns to Loma's neighborhood, they think: "I would be connected to all these people if they were part of my rhizome. But here everyone is a free individual" (259).

The story raises the question of individuality, a concept that has been central in the West. Psychologists say that we must each go through the process of individuation, of becoming an individual apart from our parents, in order to become a well-adjusted human being. The story shows, though, just how fully integrated individuality is in all human interactions, how individuality permeates our mindsets. Loma and Inri cannot agree on what "love" means precisely because they hold fundamentally different ideas about what it means to be an individual or to be a rhizome. As an individual, Loma cannot imagine that Inri would not want individual freedoms; as a rhizome, Inri cannot imagine wanting individual freedoms.

While Téllez raises the question of individual selfhood, I believe that the story also offers a take on the queer politics of assimilation. One version of queer activism argues that *We just want what straight folx want. We want to get married, buy a house, have a kid.* Another version of queer politics argues that *We want to rethink that whole paradigm. We do not want to replicate straight life but throw it out the window.* In the case of "Heat Death of Human Arrogance," we see the intersection and collision of two fundamentally different perspectives. Inri doesn't really want what Loma wants; Loma can't imagine that Inri isn't just like her. In the final lines of the story, Inri reminds themself that "I am like them now. Free and autonomous." But that rings hollow. Inri really doesn't want to assimilate to individuality.

As noted, our Slow Stepper™ is named Inri. The sentence introducing Inri appears by itself, on a separate line:

"My name is Inri."

In Spanish, the expression "para más inri" means "to make matters worse." And, perhaps, that is the case here. Inri does seem to think, on several occasions, that Loma and the well-meaning humans are making matters worse. Inri also wonders if the new iterations of Slow Steppers™ are making things worse. As they become more and more like humans, and become more indistinguishable from humans, is it making their situation worse? Are they losing their sense of themself? Are they becoming more individuated like human beings?

This, perhaps ironic, separation of this sentence also emphasizes Inri's name. When written in upper case, INRI is used as an abbreviation for: "Iēsus Nazarēnus, Rēx Iūdaeōrum," or, Jesus of Nazareth, King of the Jews." These initials are frequently inscribed above Christ's head on images of the Christ's crucifixion. What would it mean to read "The Heat Death of

Human Arrogance" as a religious allegory? The reference, I think, can only be read as ironic. Christ was an individual who was crucified to save individuals. Salvation is individual. Inri is no individual. The very idea makes no sense to the Slow Steppers™.

Finally, just what is the "human arrogance" that will lose all energy and dwindle into nothingness? Is our human arrogance the idea that we can produce laborers to do dangerous work off-planet? Is it the idea that we can terraform and colonize still another frontier? Is it that we as humans can persist as individuals, locked into individualism? Is it that we tell ourselves that we can know the Other? Is it that we fool ourselves into thinking that we can be selfless? Is it the notion that something, or someone, will rescue us and save us from our own greed?

In "Heat Death of the Universe," Sarah Boyle finds herself unable to cope, unable to embody and fulfill the model for a housewife and mother. She is unable to hold it *all* together. Everything ends up in a heap of smashed pieces. At the end of "Heat Death of Human Arrogance," Loma cannot cope. She states that she would rather die than continue participation in the status quo. Perhaps Inri sees such individuality as unsustainable. Inri fears that the rhizome will collapse, that they will become individual.

Long live the rhizome.

27. How Many Is Too Few?

IN 2014, FACEBOOK worked in collaboration with some LGBTQ+ advocates and came up with a new set of gender options from which Facebook users could select. At that time, they offered 54 options. By 2021, that number had increased to 71 options. Similarly, the dating site OK Cupid increased options for would-be daters. They can select from 22 gender options and 13 sexual orientations. And yet, for both of these companies, they find that users just don't feel as though they have enough options. They find that their identity is not represented.

So, that begs the question: how many gender options are enough? How many gender identities? How many sexualities? How many sets of pronouns?

A. E. Prevost (they/them) writes fiction and is a "core writer" for an "educational series on linguistics" called *The Ling Space*. In 2018, Prevost published a short story entitled "Sandals Full of Rainwater" in a special edition of *Capricious Magazine* on "gender diverse pronouns" (ed., A. C. Buchanan [they/them]). That edition of the magazine was chosen for the Honor List for the Otherwise (Tiptree) Award. (I was on the jury that selected the awards that year.) In the introduction to the issue, Buchanan writes that the English language has two gender pronouns, but that "Humans don't always fit into these boxes" (8).

"Sandals Full of Rainwater" takes place in an unknown time and place. We know that there are two cities, Salphaneyin and Orpanthyre. In the former, they speak Tisalpha, and in the latter, they speak Orpan. The key difference here is the ways in which they each handle gender and pronouns.

In the story, Piscrandiol leaves the drought-stricken city of Salpaheyin and arrives in the rainy city of Orpanthyre. They miss a connection with a relative and find themself at a boarding house. When they meet a family outside with no place to go, they suggest that the family stay with them. Piscrandiol settles down with parents Gislen, Annat, and Refe, and children Appi and Tafis. Before long, Piscrandiol has become part of the family and begun a sexual/romantic relationship with Gislen.

However, Piscrandiol finds themself overwhelmed by Orpan pronouns. They had studied them back home, but the system never made sense. They sort of knew the rules but are perpetually flummoxed in practice. In Orpan, they use three grammatical genders, in three cases. The genders, however, are not based on the sex or genitals of the speaker, but, rather, "some sort of internal social sense of being" (2018, 82). As Piscrandiol notes, "whatever gender" they had "changed depending on who they were talking to" (82). Orpan has 45 pronouns; Tisalpha has 9. In the interview with the author that follows the story, Prevost notes that they have worked out the complete Orpan gender system, but they will not reveal how it works nor what all the pronouns are (108-09).

The foundations of gender in Orpan, the number of pronouns, their shifting usage leaves Piscrandiol at a loss. In Piscrandiol's native city, they use no gender. "Our culture doesn't present [gender] at *all*" (97). Piscrandiol tells Gislen. Being gendered at every moment makes Piscrandiol uncomfortable. They hate that other people make assumptions about their gender at every moment, in every interaction. Gislen tells them, "It's just how we work" (98).

In a moment of despair, Piscrandiol rushes into the bathroom and cuts off "two feet" of red hair. They then ask, "So now? Am I different pronouns now?" (99) Gislen does stumble with the pronouns, but says it does not matter. Gislen loves Piscrandiol.

Two things happen. Piscrandiol's cousin Geloul returns, and they discover that Geloul is fluent in Orpan's gendered pronouns. Also, when Piscrandiol admits to Gislen that they feel like a burden, Gislen tries to address Piscrandiol in Tisalpha pronouns—and gets them all wrong!

"Sandals Full of Rainwater" illustrates both the arbitrariness of gendered pronouns *and* the profound effect they have on people. Two cultures and two languages handle gendered pronouns completely differently. One language (Tisalpha) makes no gender distinction; everyone is "they." Piscrandiol suggests that that means that Tisalpha speakers are not reading others for clues of gender; they are not attuned to those markers of gender that we unconsciously look for: clothing, hair, body shape, secondary sex characteristics, tone of voice, etc. Certainly they look at one another with a discerning eye. They may look for characteristics that they find desirable and attractive. But those characteristics are not tied to gender or sex.

On the other hand, the other language (Orpan) makes multiple gender distinctions; everyone has a gender. However, Orpan gender operates differently from the one we are familiar with. They read a body for gender, but it has nothing to do with sex. They address a body as gendered, but which pronoun they will use also has to do with the relationship to the speaker. With their 45 personal pronouns, Orpan speakers must constantly be aware of the gender characteristics of the person with whom they are speaking, even if the sex of that speaker seems largely irrelevant.

In Shade 14, I wrote of Ursula K. Le Guin's *The Left Hand of Darkness*. Although Le Guin defended her use of a universal masculine pronoun initially, she later agreed that she *should* have used a non-gendered pronoun to refer to the Gethenians. What reading *Left Hand* in 2021 reveals is how much the gendered pronouns overdetermine our reading of Estraven. Because Genly Ai uses "he" to describe Estraven, we the readers cannot help but be influenced in how we think of Estraven (and Gethenians). It also reveals how much we need to reconsider how we gender one another and what pronouns we use.

Prevost's "Sandals Full of Rainwater" further complicates the relationship between bodies and pronouns. The two languages in the story represent two tendencies in English. One tendency is to multiply gender categories and terms until everyone finds themselves represented. The other tendency is to get rid of the distinction altogether, so that everyone is "they." In the former model, everyone has their own box. Furthermore, that box is fluid and unfixed. In the latter model, no one has to make a choice, and the relationship between social body (gender) and the physical body (sex) is broken down. Even so, I would not suggest that Prevost favors one system over the other. Both systems have limitations. Perhaps that is a limitation of language itself.

The difficulty in "Sandals" is that each of the two characters, Piscrandiol and Gislen, were raised into one of two systems. For each one of them, the system seems natural and comfortable; for each one, the *other* system feels uncomfortable and discriminatory. Gender and gendered pronouns have an effect on us. They shape our sense of self. They shape our interpretation of others. They shape how others see us.

Keep that in mind the next time you introduce yourself, or someone takes the risk and introduces themself along with their pronouns.

28. From the Space of Compassion

> *Destroy. That's the brief of this issue. Destroy science fiction. Why? Because disabled people have been discarded from the narrative, cured, rejected, villainized. We've been given few options for our imaginations to run wild within the parameters of an endless sky. This issue destroys those narratives and more.*
>
> —Elsa Sjunneson and Dominik Parisien, "Disabled People Destroy Science Fiction"

BEGINNING IN JUNE 2014, *Lightspeed Magazine* published special issues dedicated to the proposition of "destroying" genre fiction. They published "Women Destroy Science Fiction" in 2014, followed by "Queers Destroy Science Fiction" in June 2015, and "People of Colour Destroy Science Fiction" in June 2016. (They also "destroyed" Fantasy and Horror. All of these can be found at Destroy SF.)

In 2016, the "Destroy" project was handed over to the editors at *Uncanny Magazine*, and they published " Science Fiction" in 2018. In this issue, the stories, poems, reprints, and essays feature characters of a wide range of identities and abilities. The issue includes works by Rachel Swirsky (she/her), Nisi Shawl (they/them), Judith Tarr (she/her), Karin Tidbeck (they/them), Rose Lemberg (they/them), Sarah Gailey (they/them), and many others. Among the fiction contents is a short piece by Merc Fenn Wolfmoor (they/them) a queer/nonbinary writer (who has also published material as A. Merc Rustad).

In this story, Kaityn Falk (they/them) is agender, "autistic and hyperempathic." Consequently, Kaityn feels uncomfortable on Earth, around the teeming millions of other people and so works for the Galactic Exploration for Peace (GEP) agency, setting research beacons throughout deep space for the purposes of star-charting. They are a million miles from anyone else, and they couldn't be happier. Their only companion is an AI pilot called Horatio.

On a routine mission on Io 7, they (Kaityn and Horatio) detect something on their scanners, and Kaityn quickly senses something, or someone, in pain. Kaityn walks on the moon surface and finds a lifeform that has crashed. However, a rival company has also tracked the signal, and the representatives intend to take the alien for study. They will not listen to Kaityn, and they fire their weapons at her. The alien immobilizes the threat, saving Kaityn's life. Kaityn says they are now even.

The story raises a number of important issues: confronting Otherness, identity, and compassion.

The lifeform seems wholly Other to Kaityn. They describe it as "octagonal light" with "rippling edges, "two feet in diameter" with no appendages. The lifeform has no verbal language but communicates via empathic sensations. It is alone and in pain, separated from its whole self. In this sense, the alien is the opposite of Kaityn, who feels pain at being in the whole of humanity. The burst of pain knocks Kaityn over; Horatio fears they are dead. The alien lifeform apologizes for the assault, and, significantly, Horatio can also hear the communication. But through this very direct communication, Kaityn now knows the alien's gender and pronouns (nu/nur). Kaityn and the alien are profoundly different, and yet, they share the value of life and the beauty of space.

At the end of the encounter, the alien is reunited with its whole self, and Kaityn with Horatio. Once the alien lifeform is gone, Kaityn realizes that they have treated Horatio as something other than a life form. They discover that Horatio had been programmed "male," but prefers to use "ze/zir" pronouns.

As noted, Kaityn's identity and ability are central to why and how they connect to the alien. In a flashback, we learn that a previous boyfriend had questioned Kaityn's suitability to act as first contact. "Wouldn't being agender just confuse them?" The now-ex-boyfriend had assumed that aliens would be bigender, just as he really thought humans are (should be) bigender, as well. Horatio tells Kaityn that her ex had held them back from being their "true self."

Kaityn had wondered if aliens would have gender at all, let alone two of them. In fact, the alien makes no assumptions about gender. Kaityn does learn the pronouns used by the alien, but we learn nothing more about the alien's sexual or gender identity (assuming they are even separate). No, Kaityn's identity and their being are precisely what makes the interaction work.

Because of who they are, because they are autistic and hyperempathethic, Kaityn senses the alien crash, feels the alien's pain, and communicates with the alien. The story's title gets at this relationship: the frequency of compassion. In one sense, Kaityn seems to be on the same wavelength as the alien (as is Horatio). The other humans seem insensate, on the wrong wavelength. In another sense, how *often* do we offer or receive such acts of compassion? For Kaityn, what were disabilities on Earth (autism and hyperempathy) are precisely what allow them to succeed with the alien. That "disability" is the key to compassion. In this reversal, Wolfmoor queers our expectations and understanding of "disability."

The issue of *Uncanny* promised to "destroy" the usual narratives of SF and to make "disabled people" visible, to center them in the stories. In this case, an agender person with autism and a gender-nonconforming AI are front and center.

Furthermore, their identities are not superficial but integral to the whole plot and resolution.

Destroying these outmoded preconceptions seems about right.

29. The Heretic Has Left the Building

CANADIAN ADA HOFFMAN (she/her) is an Adjunct Professor of Computer Science. Hoffman was diagnosed with Asperger's when she was 13 and is a dedicated autism advocate. Indeed, she has hosted the online Autistic Book Party since 2012(ish). Her short story "Minor Heresies" appeared in *Ride the Star Wind*, a collection of Lovecraft-inspired pieces, edited by C. Dombrowski (he/him) and Scott Gable (he/him). The story was then collected in *Transcendent 3* (ed., Bogi Takács, 2018).

In "Minor Heresies," (some) far-future humans have been melded with alien "filigree." Initially designed and grown in vats at Vaur Station, later iterations of these "Vaurians" are grown outside the lab, with parents. The human-grown Vaurians can be "men, women, neither, both, and in between." The alien filigree allows them to shift their shape limitlessly. Some Vaurians then become "angels," who are used to terraform other planets, to organize society, or to hunt down "heretics." The angels report to the "Gods," which are sentient AIs that reign over human space.

At first glance, Vaurian sex seems to affirm the diversity of human sex. While popular "knowledge" clings to the notion that humans are either one of two sexes, science and medicine have long noted that that simply isn't true. The term "intersex" has recently given way to "Disorders of Sex Development" (see Shade 11) to describe the myriad number of situations that result in nature (though some within the community prefer "*Differences* of Sex Development," for obvious reasons).

For some, the shortcoming of the term "intersex" was that some intersex individuals identify as female or male, and so the term left them out. For others, the difficulty was that the term seemed to assume that female and male were "the sexes" and that intersex existed in between the two "real" sexes. Here, Hoffman offers "neither, both, and in between." And, yet, the inclusion of "men, women" unintentionally reinforces the belief that male and female are norms against which all other sexes are defined.

Enter Mimoru, among the first generation of Vaurians to be grown outside the lab. Mimoru, however, flunks out of angel school. He doesn't have what it takes. He prefers to sit and read. So, a Vaurian who cannot be an angel must find a job. Mr. Haieray of the Stardust Interplanetary Trading Company hires Mimoru to be an accountant. However, Mr. Haieray has other plans, and he compels Mimoru to use his shapeshifting skills in order to woo clients. Haieray also employs a number of nonhumans in order to appeal to alien trading partners. He treats them just as poorly. For example, Bûr-Nïb, a secretary in the company, a bipedal humanoid from Ìntlànsûr frequently bears the ire of Haieray.

For Haieray, Mimoru is an Other, someone to be mistrusted and abused. While the Vaurians are frequently a weapon of the Gods, Mimoru has failed. But then, "Nobody wanted a shifty, unpredictable shapechanger" (181) working for them. Mimoru's ability to change bodily shape, including changing sex, is simply a tool for Haieray's exploitation. Haieray mistreats Mimoru and Bûr-Nïb because they are not human, because they do not conform to human norms, and because they are aliens in human space/business.

On their latest business venture, Haieray, Mimoru, and Bûr-Nïb travel to Hex Station to trade with the Zora, who "resemble horse-sized insects made of beads: heads, joints, and legs made of spherical segments, alternately pitch-black and chalk-white" (182). The Zora also hold particular religious practices, which do not conform to human practices. Haieray compels Mimoru to change into a shape more pleasing to the Zora, including a change of sex. She complies.

The AI, also known as the "human Gods," aggressively cut off all contact with outside belief systems and practices. They allow no information about nature worship, spiritual beings, or alternate philosophies. If a human (or Vaurian) came to believe what an alien believed, they would be a "heretic" and subject to execution. But when the Zora leave the negotiations to return to quarters, Haieray orders Mimoru to change shape (again) and follow them. Never mind that that's espionage. Never mind that they might also be engaged in some religious practice forbidden to humans (and Vaurians). Haieray wants his sale.

When Mimoru tracks the Zora to their quarters, he gets a momentary glimpse of their religious ceremony. He glimpses a large being, larger than an entire galaxy, eyes as large as stars. The Zora shut it off as quickly as he can register the scene, but the damage has been done. Had it been real? An hallucination? The doctor says he is not crazy, only "a mild Asperger neurotype" (186). Instead, the doctor diagnoses "heresy." He now has the knowledge, if not the active belief, that something exists in the universe that is larger and more powerful than the Gods.

The Gods will execute him.

The official propaganda of the Gods taught all children, all citizens that "heretics" slit people's throats and blow up buildings. In training to be an angel, Mimoru also learns of "minor heresies": believing the wrong things.

In the end, the Íntlànsûran Bûr-Nib rescues Mimoru. She notes that he is "not really one of them" (190). She—and nearly every other alien race—sees humans as part of a "theocratic homicidal cult" (190). Mimoru has "failed" as a human. What does that mean? Mimoru cannot simply deceive others for his own benefit; Mimoru cannot help but see things from others' perspectives; Mimoru cannot share the human-centered view of the universe. And so, he has failed.

Mimoru notes that he must stop judging others based on the standards of humans—a species that does not even want him—and start judging himself and others by his own standards. What does this mean for a queer person?

In "Minor Heresies," Hoffman offers an individual outside the norms of acceptability. Mimoru shifts shape, changes bodies, and moves among sexes regularly. Mimoru has no fixed sex or gender identity. But Mimoru has been trying to make sense of his life and the lives of others, based on a set of norms developed by those in power. Those norms have failed Mimoru and have failed humanity.

Of course, one answer is to change the norms. To stay and challenge them and to get people to begin to see things differently. Mimoru, though, has a (metaphorical and literal) gun at his temple. So, he flees. The only space for Mimoru is outside of human space, or whatever currently passes for human.

Is Hoffman overly pessimistic? "Minor Heresies" seems to suggest that humans and humanity will not change any time soon, will not be able to accommodate difference, so the only answer is to flee. Like Ruth and Althea Parsons in James Tiptree's "The Women Men Don't See," who would rather flee with aliens than remain on Earth, Mimoru jumps on a ship with Bûr-Nib. And, yet, the aliens here represent groups of people and individuals who DO see things differently, who do have a different set of norms, who are outside the awful human biases and limitations.

And in that sense, I read "Minor Heresies" as hopeful.

30. Asexual Self-Love

> *I bought you mail order*
> *My plain wrapper baby*
> *Your skin is like vinyl*
> *The perfect companion*
>
> —Bryan Ferry/Roxy Music,
> "In Every Dream Home a Heartache"

SEX DOLLS ARE not new. Roxy Music sang of the mind-blowing pleasures of a blow-up sex doll in "In Every Dream Home a Heartache" (1973). In 1996, Abyss Creations began offering RealDoll sex dolls, which feature life-like, customizable dolls that do not require inflation. Anna Kendrick (she/her) stars in *Dummy* (2020), a delightful comedy in which she steals her boyfriend's sex doll. They take a road trip, talk about personal and professional matters, but have no sex. The RealDoll has been upgraded to Realdoll^x, which offers an AI-driven modular head that allows movement and verbal interaction. In a more recent competition, Robot Companion AI offers similar features. The company claims that their sex dolls feature "integrate internet technology, voice interactive system, sensing technology, mechanical and electrical integration technology" ("About Us"). They "aim to bring you conversations that you enjoy whilst having the ability to be more intimate than you have before with a human" ("About Us"). Indeed.

But one of the things about sex dolls is that they have tended to be pretty heteronormative. Who buys them? For what purposes? What are their aesthetics? RealDoll, for example, offers 33 interchangeable faces for its female dolls, all of which conform to social norms of attractiveness. It offers 11 body types, in 5 different heights, and in 5 skin tones. RealDoll used to offer a male doll, but he seems to have disappeared from the site. They do, however, offer a number of lifelike penises.

So, what would a queer sex doll look like? Or, more to the point, what would a queer take on sex dolls be?

Sarah Kanning (she/her) wrote five SF stories between 2008 and 2012. Her short story "Sex with Ghosts" first appeared in *Strange Horizons* in August of 2008. It was reprinted in *Beyond Binary: Genderqueer and Sexually Fluid Speculative Fiction* (2011, ed., Brit Mandelo).

Imagine a future in which the RealDoll and the Robot Companion have been upgraded. Imagine that the sex dolls can look exactly like anyone: celebrity, entertainer, politician, historical figure. Imagine that the services of these devices could be purchased from a reputable establishment. Imagine having a line of credit sufficient to get you through the door of The Boutique.

Carla works as a receptionist at The Boutique. She greets customers, takes down the details of clients' fantasies and fetishes. She's paid handsomely, in part because not everyone would be comfortable fielding such questions. Plus, Carla doesn't mind since she is asexual.

For decades, people spoke of heterosexual, homosexual, and bisexual. Rarely did they mention asexual. Not asexual as in the reproductive strategy of an amoeba, but rather asexual as in having no desire for sex with anyone of any sex or gender. In the past decade, though, more attention has been paid to asexuality. One key difficulty is finding a way to define and talk about asexuality without describing it as a *lack:* a *lack* of desire, the *absence* of desire, *not* hetero- or homo-. All of those options assume that having sexual desire is the norm and that asexual is somehow a failure of desire.

And, yet, Carla works happily enough in The Boutique, with no temptation to sample any of the goods. And she deftly and wittily fends off all advances by her smitten co-worker. However, Carla does undermine and challenge the heteronormative nature of the sex industry. She pooh-poohs the sex with exes, the sex with celebrities, and the sex with minors. It's all sort of ho-hum for her. She notes that she has no idea what it would be like to exist for "physical, sexual pleasure."

One fateful day, a customer walks in and is more nervous than usual, especially for a returning customer. When he asks to speak to someone else, a red flag goes up in Carla's head. Later that day, a bot asks to speak to Carla. She turns and faces herself—the spitting image of Carla. Apparently, customers have been asking for sex with the hot receptionist. The owner of the Boutique, Jones, capitalist that he is, is only too happy to oblige.

Carla challenges him and raises the ethical questions. How can this be a thing? How can he simply usurp her likeness and sell it for sex? (She signed terms of employment.) For Carla, Jones has crossed a line. But what does it mean to create a bot in someone's likeness? Do they own their likeness? Perhaps, if they are a celebrity; unlikely, if they are a receptionist. If the robot only shares an appearance but not memories or personality, then is it less of a violation? Should Carla have some reasonable sense of privacy at work? She argues that any and every customer can have sex with her likeness and then walk in the front door and leer at her. Jones counters that they all already look at her that way.

Carla steals the bot and drives to a motel in Indiana. She learns that the bot's name is Narcisse—the feminine form of Narcissus, the mythological lad who was so beautiful that he fell in love with his own reflection. The nymph Echo could not entice him away from his own image. Narcisse has many skills, including massage, counseling, and 18th- and 19th-century

English literature. While making tea, Narcisse recites a poem by W. B. Yeats, "A Coat."

The poem itself is a meta-reflection on Yeats's own process; he patches poems together from bits of this and that, from "old mythologies," but people misappropriate his work, so he lets them have it. Better to walk away naked. In the story, the Boutique has misappropriated Carla's shape. Perhaps she would be better off to let them have it and walk away naked.

Carla takes a hot shower to unwind and emerges from the bathroom to see Narcisse, on the bed, enthusiastically engaged in what sex bots do. Carla mutters, "You aren't Narcisse…just the reflection." The sex bot, Narcisse, is merely a reflection of Carla. In other words, Carla is the original, the unutterably beautiful original, full of self-love. Carla is not a narcissist; asexuality is not narcissism.

For one thing, Kanning offers a representation of an asexual individual. Very few asexual characters appear in SF/F, and representation matters. For another, Kanning treats asexuality as a legit sexuality, not as a temporary phase or a lack waiting for fulfillment. Carla remains asexual in the midst of pervasive sexual activity. Jones can misappropriate her form, but Carla remains who and what she is. But she is far from a narcissist. The clients enter the Boutique looking for something: a sexual fantasy, a desire, a fetish, a wish fulfillment, a connection to another. Something is missing. Carla offers a representation of asexuality as something whole in itself. Carla does not need the reflection, does not need Narcisse.

And she certainly does not need a RealDoll or a Robot Companion AI.

31. It Gets Better, Even in Kansas

AS THE STORY has it, Dan Savage and his partner Terry Miller began the "It gets better" movement in 2010 with a casual utterance of those three words. The words and sentiment were picked up by social media, and then became a global organization. The aim of the organization is to "uplift and empower" LGBTQ youth who might be struggling with coming to terms with their sexuality, with coming out, and with acceptance. The science fiction story "Ad Astra Per Aspera" by Nino Cipri can be read as a fictional account of "It gets better."

The story first appeared in the "Gender Diverse Pronouns" issue of *Capricious Magazine* (see Shade 27). "Ad Astra Per Aspera" is a cheeky, short piece about shifting genders and runaway pronouns. The story takes place in Kansas, mostly in a diner, and the state motto on the state logo provides the title. The phrase is Latin for "to the stars through difficulties." An archived version of the State of Kansas website notes that Kansas became the 34th state in January 1861 ("Interactive Kansas Seal," 2008). The official history of the seal claims that the motto acknowledges the difficulties that the early settlers faced, including the great race/slavery war. However, John James Ingalls (he/him), Kansas's first Secretary of the Senate, is credited with suggesting the motto. According to him, he envisioned 33 stars in the skies and one new star emerging from dark clouds, which symbolized the struggles of early statehood. The motto was adopted in May 1861 ("Kansas State Motto," 2016).

A running image in the story is the poem "Le bâteau ivre" (The Drunken Boat) by Arthur Rimbaud. He was a bit of an iconoclast and had a two-year, tumultuous relationship with fellow poet Paul Verlaine. Written in 1871 when he was just 16, the poem employs an extended nautical metaphor to represent the journey of life. A boat believes that it is breaking away from human society and floating freely—much like our narrator.

Cipri's narrator is unnamed. Since the name, gender, and pronouns are unknown, and since "x" is a variable, for the purposes of discussing the story I will employ the variable "x." In doing so, I do not mean to impose a gender or a pronoun on the narrator but only want to be able to talk about the narrator as a variable, as a potential, which I think reinforces the point of the story. X is driving through Kansas and musing on all the things x has lost on road trips: a journal, a bag, a wallet, and a gender. The narrator imagines that a waitress in a diner, with a nametag that says "Debra," might have picked up a lost book or a lost gender, that she might be contemplating a name change or a pronoun change.

The ponderings about gender in Kansas are peppered with proleptic parentheses. The narrator frequently pauses to allow the reader space to contemplate their own preconceptions and assumptions: about Kansas, about the narrator, about losing one's gender, about changing one's gender. Maybe, just maybe, you are not quite as sure in your gender as you thought you were. Maybe, just maybe, things can be different. Maybe they will get better.

Kansas does not have a stellar record regarding gender and queer rights. The Movement Advancement Project (MAP) tracks gender and sexual equity state by state. Regarding Kansas's Sexual Orientation Policy and Gender Identity Policy, Kansas scores "low" in both ("Kansas' Equality Profile," 2021). While same-sex marriage is allowed, the partner of a same-sex parent cannot adopt. While Kansas has some non-discrimination employment laws, it also has localities that have banned anti-discrimination laws. Non-discrimination laws tend not to apply to queer and trans youth. Further, Kansas has a number of religious exemption laws that allow discrimination of queer and trans individuals. And now, in 2021, Kansas has joined the cavalcade of states working to discriminate against trans individuals and trans athletes (Bernard and Hoover, 2021).

And, yet, Cipri sets their story in Kansas. As Cipri notes, for many people, the first association with Kansas is *The Wizard of Oz*. People see Kansas as a fantasy land in which wishes can come true. They think of a magical place in which the nasty evil people can be eliminated (with flying houses or buckets of water). And, yet, Kansas has a poor record for queer and trans folx. And it is here that the narrator loses xer gender, which might be picked up and tried on by Debra. If Kansas's motto is "Ad astra per aspera," then it suggests that things can get better after, or through, or because of adversity and struggle, a Latin version of "It gets better."

To be sure, the "It gets better" movement has its detractors. The primary objection is that the sentiment does not really foreground action NOW, does not emphasize relieving pain and torment NOW. For some kids, some later moment in life is too late. But for some individuals, knowing that amazing things can happen, even in Kansas, is lifesaving. They know that things will get better, through difficulty.

The stars are possible.

32. Breaking the Binary

Here in the United States, producing and reinforcing the binary begins quite early. The process begins in kindergartens and elementary schools. The kids are lined up with boys on one side and girls on the other. They are given lists of words and asked to find each word's "pair" or its "opposite." The former practice reinforces an "us versus them" mentality, *and* it reinforces the notion that gender is a salient and defining factor in their lives. The latter exercise teaches them to think in binary terms (literally and figuratively), *and* it trains them to think simplistically. But nature rarely works in a binary.

Some will argue that binary thinking *is* natural. After all, we have two eyes, two hands, two arms, two legs, etc. One left, one right. We may have two arms, but the idea that they are opposites is a social construct. Two does not necessarily mean opposite. Some will also argue that nature gives us two sexes, female and male. This claim is also false and just as much a social construct; science and medicine make clear, sex comes in a wide range of options (see Shade 9).

Current science may not imagine quite as many as Cynthia Ward does. Ward (she/her) may be best known for her work with Nisi Shawl on their "Writing the Other" workshops. The two authors published a short book under that title in 2005 (Aqueduct Press); fifteen years later, the book was given a Special Award from *Locus* in 2020 to acknowledge its importance in contemporary SF representation. Later, Shawl, Ward, and K. Tempest Bradford (she/her) created a series of workshops available online at *Writing the Other*. On the WtO website, they write:

> Representation is fundamental to writing great fiction. Creating characters that reflect the diversity of the world we live in is important for all writers and creators of fictional narratives. But writers often find it difficult to represent people whose gender, sexual orientation, racial heritage, or other aspect of identity is very different from their own. This can lead to fear of getting it wrong—horribly, offensively wrong—and, in the face of that, some think it's better not to try.

Bradford, Shawl, and Ward, however, take the position that representation is "too important to ignore." All writers can and should represent a wide range of characters, even if those characters don't look or act or think just like the author. Writers *must* write the Other.

Ward herself has written a lot of short stories. Her first story appeared in 1991, with the most recent appearing in 2020. "Body Drift" appeared in the November/December 2018 issue *Analog Science Fiction and Fact*. It was nominated for the Otherwise (Tiptree) Award that year and received an Honorable Mention.

"Body Drift" takes the form of a conversation between the narrator and an unseen interlocutor. From the very first sentence, Ward signals that she will rewrite the traditional narrative:

> Once upon a future to come, a boy and girl fell in love.

Instead of the familiar "Once upon a time," Ward shifts it to the future, even as she simultaneously suggests that it will be a traditional love story. No, she quickly confesses that she is lying about that. The relationship has no traditional elements whatsoever.

Instead, we learn that the boy is a "boi" and that "he" (just using a pronoun that we would recognize) has had every single possible part of his body replaced. He now takes the form of a 20-foot-tall Moebius strip, with no limbs (unless he wants them) and no sex organs (unless he wants them). The girl has similarly had most of her body replaced: organs, appendages, blood, digestive system, and brain.

They both embody genders that we would not recognize. They both have names that we cannot pronounce, though for the purposes of this story they are called Friedrich and Fuschia. Here, though, I would argue that Ward has fallen into the same trap that Ursula K. Le Guin (she/her) did in *The Left Hand of Darkness*. Le Guin's choice to use the universal masculine pronoun to refer to the Gethenians, a race without a permanent sex or gender, trapped the reader into seeing the Gethenians, in general, and Estraven, in particular, as *men* (see Shade 14). For convenience, Ward also uses "he" and "she," to similar effect.

Nevertheless, in constructing these two characters, Ward attempts to break the binary (even while demonstrating how difficult that is—and by that I mean occasionally slipping back into terms or ways of thinking even as she is trying to break free of them). She notes that sex is multiple. She argues that the future acknowledges more genders than colors seen by a tetrachromat (100,000,000). More importantly, she attempts to rupture the body-gender connection. Whatever bodies Fuschia and Friedrich were born into do not matter. For one, those bodies have been radically altered. They bear little resemblance to the bodies they were born into, and they bear little resemblance to anything we might describe as "human." More importantly, they face no social approbation for doing so. For another, their gender expression is clearly separate and apart from their bodies. The old argument that gender is based on our bodies is destroyed. Simone de Beauvoir makes the argument quite strongly in 1949 in *Le deuxième sexe* that gender is not, and cannot be, predicated upon the body. Ward's 2018 science fiction story deftly illustrates the point. The "body is not a thing but rather a situation" (de Beauvoir).

The deconstructed fairy tale continues: the two "meet," though in no conventional sense. They just happen to meet in the exact same virtual space in the exact same femtosecond (that's 1x10 to the 15th power). In that instant, they recognize their compatibility. They marry and produce an offspring (virtual) within a fraction of a second. And then never see one another again, as long as they both shall live. Fear not, though, you romantics: they exchange a complete set of memories of the other. Each will carry the other with them for as long as they both shall live.

So two people meet in virtual space, in bodies that bear no resemblance to the human form or to their former form. It is a meeting of the minds, and they produce a brainchild that lives on virtually. They never see one another again.

Given all that, how do we read this new-found flexibility and possibility? Is Ward suggesting an opening up of possibilities? Or is she engaged in transphobia? Are the new bodily forms a liberation or a rejection?

I have written elsewhere that the simple addition of sex or gender or sexuality categories is insufficient (see Shade 27; see also Wendy Gay Pearson). For example, although Melissa Scott's (she/her) *Shadow Man* (1995) features five sexes and nine sexualities, that proliferation is not sufficient for categorizing everyone's sex or gender identity. Here, Ward offers 100 million genders. Does that work any better? Or does it suggest that people can use just as many categories as they would like, regardless of how large the number is? Would that resolve questions of representation and inclusion?

The two areas in which I think the story comes up short are in tone and binary language. Because the story takes the form of an imagined conversation with someone not well versed in sex/gender/sexuality, it can come off as a bit condescending to the imagined interlocutor. If the story positions the reader as the imagined conversant, then it could be off-putting to the very people who need to read it. On the other hand, for those readers who are in the know about issues of gender/sex/sexuality, it can read as a bit dismissive.

In addition, as noted above, Ward does fall back into some anachronistic binary language at times. For one, the romance consists of two people, not three or eleven. Moreover, in describing Friedrich's "bio-body," Ward writes that "you" (the imagined conversant/reader) "might have said, *She's all woman*" (171). Shortly after, the narrator calls gender fluidity: "a difficult concept, for most men of our era. Most women, too" (171). But "our era" presumably refers to the time of the narrator, and in this future time this binary has been eliminated. Still, the default man/woman creeps in here. When Ward describes Fuschia's name, she writes that "it's pretty and feminine enough to suit your [the imagined reader, again] tastes" (171). In this example, it reinforces the reader's biases (Le Guin, again).

And yet, intentional fallacy aside, I do not think that Ward intends to dismiss the importance or freedom offered by such transformative technologies. In this future fairy tale, every single person can take any bodily form they want, and they can describe themselves by any terms or pronouns they like, many of which are unrepresentable in the language we are now using. That is an idea that seems to resonate today (2021)—unlimited flexibility and mutability in bodily and gender expression. Such an unlimited future would seem to fulfill the hopes and aspirations of feminist and LGBTQ activists in the here and now.

A fairy tale for the ages....

33. The Age of Destruction

> *Yeah, my blood's so mad feels like coagulatin'*
> *I'm sitting here just contemplatin'*
> *I can't twist the truth, it knows no regulation*
> *Handful of senators don't pass legislation*
> *And marches alone can't bring integration*
> *When human respect is disintegratin'*
> *This whole crazy world is just too frustratin'*
>
> *And you tell me*
> *Over and over and over again, my friend*
> *Ah, you don't believe*
> *We're on the eve*
> *of destruction.*
>
> —Barry McGuire, "The Eve of Destruction"

IN 1965, BARRY MCGUIRE (he/him) released the single, "Eve of Destruction." In the song, McGuire's gravelly voice calls out one injustice after another, one indignation after another, and repeatedly asks how anyone can doubt that we are on the eve of destruction. While McGuire catalogs the injustices of world, he makes no call to action. Despite its dire tone and message, it was an enormous success. It displaced the Beatles and stood atop the charts for 11 weeks. And, yet, that was 56 years ago, and we're still standing.

In "The Lawless," a three-part series of stories by Merc Fenn Wolfmoor, they also invoke another song from 1965, "The Sound of Silence" by Paul Simon (he/him) and Art

Garfunkel (he/him). That song was released in late '65 and similarly became a huge success. The song, in an understated, folky way, makes a call to action. Wolfmoor, however, cites the 50th anniversary cover of "The Sound of Silence" by the metal band, Disturbed. In this version, the lead singer, David Michael Draimon (he/him), channels all the rage of 50 years of inaction. He fairly screams at the listener:

> "Fools," said I, "You do not know
> Silence like a cancer grows
> Hear my words that I might teach you
> Take my arms that I might reach you."

Draimon is angry AF, and he wants all of you "fools" to listen, to speak up, and to DO something. Merc Fenn Wolfmoor has heeded these words.

The three linked stories by Wolfmoor appear in a trilogy of anthologies, collectively called the Dystopia Triptych (2020). All edited by John Joseph Adams, Christie Yant, and Hugh Howey, they feature a story by the same set of writers in all three books. Each writer was tasked with writing a story before, during, and after dystopia. Further, each book has a subtitle, taken from classic dystopian novels by George Orwell (he/him), Ray Bradbury (he/him), and Margaret Atwood (she/her).

Wolfmoor's first story, "Trust in the Law, for the Law Trusts in You," picks up in the midst of a plague of gun violence and governmental inaction. The official response is largely to push a remote, VR technology (VISIONS) so that students can go to school without the threat of violence. The authorities, however, make a gun attack in VR appear as though it were a real-world event and use that event to further impose restrictive measures. They take no action, however, on restrictive gun laws. All of which prompts a trans student, Arren Darden, to take action. He refuses to perpetuate the lies of the authorities, and he becomes a hacker and Public Enemy Number One.

In the second story, "Believe in the Law, for the Law Believes in You," the VISIONS platform has become ubiquitous and compulsory. Under this now totalitarian state (think the Republic of Gilead with more technology), Marley Leighton struggles with demons from her past—her relationships, her abortion, her tubal ligation, and her hacker past. Her husband, Joel, is a true believer, and she knows that he would never accept her secrets. When someone from the resistance contacts her, she sees a way out. They ask her to capitalize on the work that Arren has already done and to disappear some people from the database. After she deletes them—and herself—she feels finally free.

The third installment is entitled "The Law Is the Plan, the Plan Is Death." This third title clearly channels the Nebula Award-winning story by James Tiptree, Jr., "Love Is the Plan, the Plan Is Death" (1973). In Tiptree's story, a spider-like creature wants to break free from the instincts of his species that lead to violence. Although Moggadeet devises a Plan, he fails. He is killed and eaten. No. Way. Out. In Wolfmoor's story, Eleazar works for the governmental agency that tracks and monitors all citizens. His boss, Isaac, reveals that he knew Arren Darden, and that he had hoped to make a difference. He has failed. After Isaac's suicide, Eleazar has Isaac's clearance codes. When he's approached in a chat by Arren Darden and his associates, he's asked to make a choice and to wipe out the entire tracking and monitoring system. Can Eleazar defeat the Plan? Is there a way out?

In each story, the plot rests on a non-conforming character. Arren Darden is one of the few characters that appears in all three stories. As a trans student in high school, he faces many of the issues that trans kids face today—acceptance, bullying, crushes, bodily betrayals, and exploitation. Arren notes that his realization that he was trans was liberating. It was a step to see the world differently and to act accordingly. Marley has run away from her past relationships with other women and understands that she cannot run away from that part of herself any more. It causes too much harm. Eleazar has a similar realization. As Arren (and others) press Eleazar to destroy the system, the latter understands that he has not felt comfortable as a "he" for a long time. The rebels give him the space to say that he is nonbinary, that "he" is "they." He deletes the system; he defeats the Plan.

In the Hebrew Bible, Eleazar is the son of the High Priest, Aaron (read: Arren). He also played a role during the Jews' Exodus from Egypt. As Eleazar debates his final action, he hears the sound of a ringtone on Arren's phone. It is the opening bars of "The Sound of Silence."

> "You remember bits of the lyric to Arren's ringtone song, heard so long ago. '…disturb the sound of silence.'
>
> "You will." (2020)

In his head, the recollection of Draimon singing the lyrics of Simon and Garfunkel's song catapults him onto action.

Eleazar, the son of a high priest, has delivered the nation from slavery. He has broken the silence.

You can, too.

34. A Literal Metaphor

Oh I feel like an alien, a stranger in an alien place.

—Genesis, "Heathaze"

As noted earlier, one of the ways in which a piece of fiction functions as science fiction is by taking a metaphor and rendering it literal.

Metaphorically, one might say they feel like a stranger or an alien, and then, boom, a science fiction story drops in a seven-foot-tall green lizard from Betelgeuse that loves chess and shrimp cocktails. Or, more to the point, that alienated-feeling person is dropped into a society of seven-foot-tall aliens *on* Betelgeuse and literally becomes an alien in an alien place (see the work of C. J. Cherryh [she/her]). They are now literally a stranger in a strange land (Robert A. Heinlein [he/him]).

Or, one might suggest that they are in the wrong place, or that they are in the wrong time period. And, *boom*, an SF story whisks a character off into a different era, where the character experiences a profound sense of dis-placement. Tardises (*Dr. Who*) and transporters (*Star Trek*) make such literalizations all so handy.

Or, as a final example, someone might say that they do not feel comfortable in their own body, that they feel like their body is not an appropriate place for who they are. And, boom, we get a story in which the protagonist shifts into a new body, a new sex, a new gender. They upload their stored consciousness into an AI (Pat Cadigan [she/her]), or they shift into a newly grown clone body (John Varley).

175

Or, they become an attack helicopter. This one might take a bit of explaining....

As has been documented in a lot of places on the web, the "I sexually identify as an attack helicopter" meme appeared in either 2006 or 2014. Although "credit" usually goes to an online user named Guuse who posted the statement in 2014, there *is* a variation of it that appeared in 2006 when a troll tried to stump an online computer guide by claiming to be a "furry" whose fursona was an "Apache helicopter." Whether Guuse was aware of the earlier instance is unclear. What is clear is that its usage skyrocketed after the Guuse post (Winnington, 2015).

Guuse made the statement as a way to discredit narratives and discussions about gender identity, in general, and trans narratives, in particular. It was a way for Guuse to belittle the idea that someone could "become" a different gender. The block of text was copied-and-pasted into discussions about gender identity (a copypasta). The text also built in a "failsafe" by claiming that anyone who could not accept Guuse's new gender as an Apache helicopter was a "heliphobe."

As memes, by definition, do, the copypasta took on a life of its own. Dozens of variations appeared in which people claimed to identify as some inanimate object, including a Pringles chip, a minion, and a ghost pirate ship. The use of the meme appeared to peak in 2015 (memes tend to have short shelf lives), though it still pops up from time to time.

Enter Isabel Fall (she/her). In January 2020, Fall published a story in *Clarkesworld* magazine entitled "I Sexually Identify As an Attack Helicopter." It was, as far as I have been able to determine, Fall's first and only story. The fallout was swift. While some readers enjoyed or appreciated the story, just as many did not. They felt that the story was inappropriate, that it perpetuated a harmful meme, or that it was written by someone who just did not understand trans identity.

As a partial response, Fall identified herself as a trans woman. The bio that appeared with the story said very little and provided very few details about Fall's identity. That was on purpose. The strategy is common enough for trans individuals who do not want to risk being publicly identified as trans. In the midst of claims that Fall must have been writing from a cis-het perspective and death threats, Fall felt compelled to come out as trans. The coercion was only partially successful. Hate and threats continued, and Fall finally asked editor and publisher Neil Clarke to pull the story from the magazine site. In addition, Fall donated payment for the story to charity. The story link was replaced by a statement from Clarke, explaining why he removed the story from the site (2020). Clarke also takes some responsibility for not preparing and supporting Fall better.

What caused the furor?

In the story itself, which sometimes gets overlooked amidst all the controversy, the protagonist is Barb (think razor wire and nails). Barb is military woman who has transitioned into a new body and a new gender—as an attack helicopter. The reassignment surgery fundamentally alters a number of aspects about Barb. Now, Barb and the machine have a kind of symbiotic relationship. While Barb can walk around outside the helicopter (and have sex), Barb is part and parcel with the helicopter. Her senses, her sense of her self, her behavior, her goals have all been transformed. Barb's sexed body has taken on a new gendered construct.

And here we have another example of SF making the metaphor literal. Feminists, gender theorists, and queer theorists have long acknowledged that gender is a (social) construct. They have long operated on the understanding that gender is something separate and different from one's physical body.

And that's what Barb's helicopter is to her. It is the (physical) construct that contains her identity and behavior. This literalized construct also further ruptures the body/gender relationship. Barb's gender certainly cannot be predicated upon Barb's physical body.

In the story, Barb and her gunner, Axis, are out on a mission to bomb a school that has been taken over by a credit union. Here the story veers toward an essentialist argument: attack helicopters by nature are weapons of war, and they bomb stuff. Barb is a helicopter and must bomb stuff. Would the story have been more transgressive if Barb's helicopter were an instrument of peace? Perhaps, but even so....

Nevertheless, Fall does challenge the simple binary of masculine and feminine, and Barb does embody characteristics that we might call masculine and ones that we might call feminine. And as a soldier for the government, Barb is only too happy to carry out its mission. Barb feels a satisfaction in locking onto a target and taking it out; she feels sensual pleasure in outrunning the counterattacking airplane.

At the same time, Barb is concerned about Axis's apparent hesitations about bombing a school. She wonders if Axis is questioning her own gender, and Barb encourages her to pursue it.

Setting aside for the moment *real* concerns about the intentional fallacy, what did Fall set out to achieve? According to Clarke, Fall hoped to take a hurtful and damaging meme and reclaim it, to take away its power to cut. In recent years, activists have reclaimed many harmful words, resignifying them with power and self-determination (the n-word, the c-word, the b-word, the q-word). So, does Fall succeed in reclaiming the meme?

In a word, "no." Perhaps the meme itself, the notion of a helicopter as a gender, was simply irredeemable. Though I do not think that's the case. While possibly far-fetched, the construct nevertheless contains the very critique that feminist and queer theorists have argued for decades. Perhaps the meme was too well established to be resignified. This, too, seems unlikely. Consider the other terms that have been reclaimed and how long they have been established. The attack helicopter is a veritable newcomer.

No, the interesting element here is that the resistance to the resignification came largely from inside the house. The critiques (at least the ones that I've seen) were from feminist and queer writers and activists who questioned both the authenticity of the story and the function of the story.

Does it work as a story? I enjoy the story. I think it is not a flawless story, though it does have moments of absolute poetry. The concept is clever even if the execution is not quite up to it. But so what? Isn't this the very charge that has been lobbed at SF for decades: good ideas, bad writing? Then why attack this one?

So, does Fall have the authority to write this story? Although not initially identified as a trans writer, Fall did eventually make that fact known. (For those with epistemological doubts, Clarke confirms Fall's identity.) Nevertheless, since Fall was not explicitly identified as trans, many readers assumed that she is cis-het. In other words, they assumed the default—which is the very charge made against straight people who automatically assume everyone is straight. Others thought that the writing was that of a het woman, not a trans woman. Wasn't the George Eliot example enough? Or Robert Silverberg's (he/him) categorical statement that James Tiptree, Jr. could only be a man?

Fall wrote from her own experience as a trans woman. Though, as Clarke points out in his editorial, each experience as a trans person is unique and cannot stand as a universal experience. Fall wrote with good intentions. Fall wrote with some skill. Further, the story passed through "sensitivity readers." I would suggest that Fall was, indeed, authorized to write the story. Even so, does that mean that everyone can, should, or will appreciate it? In a word, "no."

Despite the backlash and protests, in December 2020, the story—now simply called "Helicopter Story"—was published as a limited-edition ebook, with all proceeds also being donated to charity. It sold out prior to publication. As further vindication, in April 2021, the story was named as a finalist for the Hugo Award for the Best Novelette.

Time will tell if the story has any lasting impact—on the meme, on our responses to stories/authors, and on the field of SF. However, I hope that Fall and others will continue to write stories that challenge the boundaries of SF representation. In other words, I hope they continue to queer SF. A white, cis-het writer can write about a whole range of characters, and yet no one puts the entire weight of cis-het representation upon their shoulders. For now, that is precisely what happens to writers like Fall—and to all writers in marginalized communities. They do not have the luxury to write whatever they like without its reflecting upon the entire community. And we need to get to a place where that is no longer the case.

I mean that literally.

35. Swedish Retail Therapy

> *But reading SF/F I think inoculated me against being too afraid of the future, and so many trans and queer people have been robbed of the opportunity to get old. I'll take the grief that's undoubtedly coming, because, I know there will be joy, too. The future's gonna be weird and messy and parts of it will probably be awful, but I genuinely want to be around to see it.*
>
> —Nino Cipri, in Mandelo, "Queering SFF"

I HAVE BEEN in an IKEA twice in my life. That was quite enough for me. As I traipsed through the hallways, through the display rooms, I recall feeling completely hemmed in and conscripted in my movements. The sensation that we were trapped, channeled forward like cattle in a slaughterhouse, was all too palpable. The second time, I was there to return something, and I knew where I needed to go to return it, but that was at the far end of the maze-that-is-IKEA. And so, we traversed the entire store once again. Damned frustrating. And I haven't even mentioned the infamous instruction booklets or the quality of the furnishings. And so, IKEA has no place in my heart.

Generally speaking, science fiction has taken two strategies in thinking about business. Some have simply taken business to be the thing that keeps the world spinning, and the thing that will spur (and finance) our journey into space. Think Robert A. Heinlein, or C. J. Cherryh, or Dani (he/him) & Eytan (he/him) Kollin. Space is the place, and corporations will get us there. Companies, not governments, will bankroll the great outward migration. Other writers have been more critical of the practices and ends of business. The drive for profits, the entrapment of consumers, the degradation of the environment for profit, the shift of governmental roles to businesses, and so on have been fodder for SF writers. They have extrapolated from current trends and drawn ominous dystopias. Think Fredrick Pohl (he/him), Max Berry (he/him) or Blythe Woolston (she/her).

With *Finna*, Nino Cipri falls into the latter category. In a former moment in their life, Cipri was a union organizer. On their website, Cipri writes of their efforts to organize workers at a national bike-share company. Through the process, Cipri learned a lot about labor relations, in general, and the company they worked for, in particular. They write:

> That's what's happening in the job market now, for working-class and lower-middle class people in America: we're expected to give everything to companies that treat us like ass, and we should be grateful to receive any kind of income at all. ("The Accidental Organizer")

Cipri writes that they took all their years of experience and all their frustrations in working for companies, and channeled them into *Finna* (a 2021 finalist for the Hugo Award for the Best Novella) ("Nino Cipri | Finna"). And, to be sure, the picture of the large chain box store is not pretty (though it is often humorous).

In the novella, Ava (she/her) reports to work at a large, IKEA-like box store called LitenVärld ("little world" in Swedish). She has just broken up with her romantic partner and hopes not to run into Jules (they/them), who also works there. But, of course, they do. As they try to maintain their distance on shift, circumstance—and crappy management—

pushes them together. You see, LitenVärld is prone to maskhål (or "wormholes"). The wormholes open up in these not-at-all-IKEA stores and people disappear into them. On this day, a woman has reported that her grandmother is missing. When the search party is assembled to find Ursula Nouri, Jules volunteers because they just can't take it anymore: the breakup, the recriminations, the misgendering, the cut-and-dried world that they just don't seem to fit into. Ava gets sent along because she has the least seniority of all the workers on shift. Thus begins their great adventure.

Ava and Jules are given a comical device, a "Finna" ("find" in Swedish), in order to track the missing grandmother. A green arrow points them in the direction of Nouri, or the next best approximation. You see, according to the infinite worlds theory, an infinite number of Ursula Nouris must exist. If they cannot find *their* Ursula Nouri, then certainly another one from another dimension would be just as good? When they discover that Nouri has, indeed, been eaten by a carnivorous chair, they move on to their next best option, sea captain Urzula Nouresh.

In the (near) infinite number of universes, a (near) infinite number of Avas and Juleses and Ursulas must exist in a (near) infinite number of LitenVärlds. The conceit bears a resemblance to the Jorge Luis Borges story "The Library of Babel," in which a very large number of books, each a slight variation of the others, exist in the library/universe. In the Library, millions of near-identical books exist scattered throughout the universe.

That theory might lead the reader to believe that a kind and benevolent version of LitenVärld must exist. In the first alternate version we see, a hive/collective bound to a voracious Mother who literally demands blood from the consumer. The palm scanner, called a "mortänder" (mother teeth) draws blood from the palm of the hand as payment. When Ava and Jules flee, the hive pursues them into another universe. Cipri suggests that capitalism will literally suck the blood out of you, will track you down, and destroy you.

But what's so queer about that? Well, nothing in particular. But Cipri is also doing something else. In every relationship, Cipri queers the possibilities. For one, the corporation codes all employees as "family," but it's a dysfunctional family at best, and a deadly family at worst. This notion of family cannot stand. The hivemind of Mother is a similarly destructive and deadly familial model. On the other hand, Uzsula Nouresh "returns" to a granddaughter from another universe whom she has never seen. Their bond is based on some weird fiction of unconventional family.

Finally, Ava, a white cis-het woman, is in a relationship with Jules, a Black, non-binary immigrant. As they try to fit their relationship into a conventional box, it fails. They are miserable. What their adventures in the multiple worlds teaches them is that a lot of other possibilities exist. They exist in a universe in which they have never met. They exist in a universe where they are married with children. They exist in a universe in which they are in queer relationships with others. They exist in a universe in which they are best friends. And so, Ava understands that she and Jules need not fit into a conventional model. They can look for other models, and they can exist outside the box(store).

Finna is funny and charming—something difficult to get right in SF. But I always wonder about the use of humor to challenge social injustice. Does turning the alienation and exploitation by corporations into a joke (Duh, Capitalism) enhance or undermine the social commentary? Does turning the horrors of corporate greed and depersonalization into an absurd Lovecraftian horror hurt or help the case against multinational corporations? While I have no general answer, in the case of *Finna*, the commentary remains after the laughter stops.

But it's all connected, isn't it? The take-down of the shitty management of a mega-corporation, the faux family feelings, the disenfranchised queer and trans employees, the Lovecraftian horrors, the wormholes, and the multiple—no, (near) infinite—possibilities of the universe are all intersectional, inter-dimensional politics on parade. Jules, the Black trans immigrant kid, doesn't fit inside the box (gender, Sweden, LitenVärld, the universe). Their relationship with Ava does not conform to conventions. As in Borges's Library, all possible combinations are possible. Everything that can exist, does exist. In Cipri's wormhole, in an alternate universe, all things are possible. And Ava and Jules will find one that works, regardless of what that is.

Maybe the universe is a Swedish smörgåsbord, after all....

36. Who You Looking At?, or How YA SF Became Intersectional

> *All my life I've wanted to go to Earth. Not to live, of course—just to see it. As everybody knows, Terra is a wonderful place to visit but not to live. Not truly suited to human habitation.*
>
> *I'm colonial mongrel in ancestry, but the Swedish part is dominant in my looks, with Polynesian and Asiatic fractions adding no more than a not-unpleasing exotic flavor. My legs are long for my height, my waist is 48 centimeters and my chest is 90—not all of which is rib cage, I assure you, even though we old colonial families all run to hypertrophied lung development; some of it is burgeoning secondary sex characteristic.*
>
> —Robert A. Heinlein, *Podkayne of Mars*

OH, WE HAD YA SF when I was young. But (a) not a lot of it, and (b) of a very different quality. I remember reading Robert Silverberg's *The Lost Race of Mars* (1960). Set in 2017, Sally and Jim must help their father determine whether or not the mummified Martians are really alive. His scientific reputation is at stake! I particularly remember reading *Podkayne of Mars* (1962-63) by Robert A. Heinlein, which involves a plucky eight-year-old (Martian years), a spaceliner to Earth, and a smuggled atomic bomb. Although a (young) female protagonist *did* push against cultural and literary norms of the day, the norms of race, ethnicity, sexuality, class, heteronormative romance and so on remained unchallenged.

But post-2010 YA SF? Well, that's a different matter.

In 2020, Alechia Dow (she/her) published her debut novel, *The Sound of Stars*. The novel dropped with a lot of hype and expectations. Dow describes herself as a Black, fat, demisexual, femme, who has mental health issues (severe anxiety). One of Dow's main purposes in writing *The Sound of the Stars* was to fill a gap in representation in YA SF. She just never saw characters like herself, and so she set out to remedy that situation. It can only remind one of something that Toni Morrison said decades earlier as she explained her reasons behind writing *The Bluest Eye* (1972).

The novel is set in a future time in which environmental degradation has seriously eroded the quality of life on Earth. On top of that, a race of aliens has arrived and quarantined human beings. The Ilori intend to clean up (read: gentrify) Earth for use as a vacation destination. Even worse, they intend to use (read: exploit, enslave) human bodies in order to experience life on Earth. They stifle human consciousness and shove it into the background while the Ilori take the human body for a spin.

The novel is structured with alternating perspectives, told from the perspective of Janelle "Ellie" Baker, a human being, and Morr1s, an Ilori. Ellie, a 17-year-old African-American girl, breaks quarantine rules and keeps a secret lending library for circulation among the enslaved humans. The consequences of being caught could be fatal. When one of her books goes missing, Ellie fears that the Ilori will trace it back to her.

Of course, the book has been taken by Morr1s, an atypical Ilori. The Ilori come in two varieties, "pure" and "labmade." Morr1s is of the latter variety. The labmade Ilori are like the Gammas and Epsilons in *Brave New World*, the azi in C. J. Cherryh's Union/Alliance universe, or the replicants in *Blade*

Runner. They are genetically engineered to perform the advance work of colonization. In this case, the labmade Ilori look like human beings and perform labor on planet Earth. And while most Ilori are not troubled much with emotions, Morr1s certainly is.

But *The Sound of Stars* is also a YA romance story, and Ellie and Morr1s are on a collision course. Like the author Dow, Ellie describes herself as demi-ace and suffers from extreme anxiety. Her medication has been withheld by the Ilori. Consequently, her attraction to Morr1s is a slow burn. Furthermore, Morr1s and the Ilori hold the power of life and death over Ellie, her family, and all humans. Individually, Morr1s tries to be respectful. He frequently asks for consent. He does not communicate telepathically without consent (unless it's life-and-death); he will not kiss her without consent. All of this discussion about consent would be valuable for young adults to read and internalize. The novel comes up short, however, in fully theorizing the structural elements of power and consent. Is consent even possible under the circumstances?

The Ilori are an invading, colonial force with superior technology. They can—and do—kill human beings for their own pleasure or convenience. Even though Morr1s himself is a bit of an iconoclast, even though Morr1s is marginal to Ilori circles of power, he still benefits from structural power. That structure gives him absolute power over Ellie, whether he elects to use it or not. A single word to authorities, and Ellie is done. He enjoys Ilori privilege by dint of being Ilori. Under those circumstances, can Ellie consent?

In addition, the novel features a demi-ace protagonist. The other half of the relationship, Morr1s, must also overcome his own programming as an unemotional and rational Ilori (read: Vulcan). And, yet, Morr1s, despite being an alien in a human body, reads much like a cis-het male. Ellie is described as demi-ace, and she does take a while to develop emotional trust for Morr1s, she eventually gets there. Because Ellie uses she/her pronouns and describes herself as feminine, the queer relationship falls a bit flat. Perhaps Dow could have pushed the boundaries of representation further if one of the protagonists had been ace?

Unlike *Podkayne of Mars*, *The Sound of Stars* does challenge a lot of cultural and generic norms. Despite the surface all-too-easy romance between two individuals alien to one another, the novel recenters representation to marginal groups. Dow has said in interviews that she *is* Ellie in a lot of ways; Dow and Ellie share a lot of identities: they are both Black, fat, demi-ace, women who struggle with mental health issues. *The Sound of Stars* asks its young readers to consider questions of colonialism, of imperialism, of gentrification, of appropriation, of ableism, of race, of sexuality, of friendship, and of love.

The Sound of Stars is not your parents' YA SF. And that's a good thing.

Primary Works Cited

Atwood, Margaret. *The Handmaid's Tale*. Ontario, Canada: McClelland and Stewart, 1985.

Brennert, Alan. "The Third Sex," *Pulphouse: The Hardback Magazine*, Issue 3, Spring 1989, 31-50.

Brissett, Jennifer Marie. *Elysium*. Seattle: Aqueduct, 2014.

Burdekin, Katherine (Murray Constantine). *Swastika Night*. London: Gollancz, 2016.

Butler, Octavia E. "Bloodchild." In *Bloodchild and Other Stories*, 3-32. New York: Four Walls Eight Windows, 1995.

Carter, Rafael. "Congenital Agenesis of Gender Ideation by K. N. Sirsi and Sandra Botkin." *Starlight 2*, edited by Patrick Nielsen Hayden, 15-29. New York: Tor, 1998.

Cipri, Nino. "The Shape of My Name." New York, Tor, 2015. https://www.tor.com/2015/03/04/the-shape-of-my-name/. Reprinted. *Transcendent: The Year's Best Transgender Speculative Fiction*, edited by K. M. Szpara, 1-16. Maple Shade, NJ: Lethe Press, 2016.

—. "Ad Astra Per Aspera." *Transcendent 4: The Year's Best Transgender Speculative Fiction*, edited by Bogi Takács, 7-9. Maple Shade, NJ: Lethe Press, 2018.

—. *Finna*. New York: Tor, 2020.

Clarke, Neil. "About the Story." *Clarkesworld*, Issue 160, January 2020. http://clarkesworldmagazine.com/fall_01_20/.

DeConnick, Kelly Sue and Valentine de Landro. *Bitch Planet*. Berkeley, CA: Image Comics, 2014.

Delany, Samuel R. "Aye, and Gomorrah." In *Dangerous Visions*, edited by Harlan Ellison, 532-544. New York: Signet, 1967.

Delliquanti, Blue. *O Human Star*, 2012-2020. https://ohumanstar.com/.

Dow, Alechia. *The Sound of Stars*. Toronto, Canada: Inkyard Press, 2020.

El-Mohtar, Amal. "To Follow the Waves." In *The Apex Book of World SF* 3, edited by Lavie Tidhar, 136-149. Lexington, KY: Apex Publishing, 2014.

Emshwiller, Carol. "Sex and/or Mr. Morrison." In *Dangerous Visions*, edited by Harlan Ellison, 326-336. New York: Signet, 1967.

Fall, Isabel. "I Sexually Identify As an Attack Helicopter." *Clarkesworld.com* January 2020. No longer available online: see https://clarkesworldmagazine.com/fall_01_20/.

Haldane, Charlotte. *Man's World*. London: Chatto and Windus, 1927.

Hoffman, Ada. "Minor Heresies." In *Transcendent 3: The Year's Best Transgender Speculative Fiction*, edited by Bogi Takács, 177-191. Maple Shade, NJ: Lethe Press, 2018.

Jemisin, N. K. *The Fifth Season*. New York: Orbit, 2015.

Jones, Gwyneth. "La Cenerentola." *Interzone* 136, October 1998, 6-14.

Kanning, Sarah. "Sex with Ghosts." In *Beyond Binary: Genderqueer and Sexually Fluid Speculative Fiction*, edited by Brit Mandelo, 205-218. Maple Shade, NJ: Lethe Press, 2011.

Kelly, James Patrick. "Lovestory." *Asimov's Science Fiction*, Vol. 1, No. 6, June 1998, 26-43.

Works Cited

Lai, Larissa. *Salt Fish Girl.* Toronto: Thomas Allan, 2002.

Lee, Tanith. *Don't Bite the Sun.* New York: DAW, 1976.

Le Guin, Ursula K. *The Left Hand of Darkness.* New York: Ace Books, 1969.

Miravete, Gabriela Damián. "And They Will Dream in the Garden." *Latin American Literature Today*, May 2018. http://www.latinamericanliteraturetoday.org/en/2018/may/they-will-dream-garden-gabriela-damián-miravete.

Monáe, Janelle. *Dirty Computer.* Emotion Pictures, April 2018. https://www.youtube.com/watch?v=jdH2Sy-BlNE.

Nieto, Tristan Alice. "Imago." In *Meanwhile, Elsewhere: Science Fiction and Fantasy from Transgender Writers*, edited by Cat Fitzpatrick and Casey Plett, 347-379. New York: Topside Press, 2017.

Orwell, George. *Nineteen Eighty-Four.* New York: Harcourt, Brace and Company, 1949.

Owomoyela, An. "God in the Sky." *Asimov's Magazine of Science Fiction*, Vol. 35, No. 3, March 2011, 50-57.

Prevost, A. E. "Sandals Full of Rainwater." *Capricious Magazine*, The Gender Diverse Pronouns Issue, Vol. 9, edited by Andi C. Buchanan, 2018, 67-114.

Romasco Moore, Maria. "The Moon Room." *Kaleidotrope*, Spring 2020, http://www.kaleidotrope.net/archives/spring-2020/the-moon-room-by-maria-romasco-moore/.

Russ, Joanna. *The Female Man.* New York: Bantam, 1975.

—. "When It Changed." In *Again, Dangerous Visions*, edited by Harlan Ellison, 248-260. New York: Doubleday, 1972.

Scott, Melissa. *Shadow Man.* New York: Tor, 1995.

Sokol, Su J. "Je me souviens." In *Glittership, Year One*, edited by Keffy K. M. Kehrli, 53-68, 2018. http://www.glittership.com/2016/02/29/episode-23-je-me-souviens-by-su-j-sokol/

Sullivan, Caitlin and Kate Bornstein. *Nearly Roadkill: An Infobahn Erotic Adventure*. New York: High Risk, 1996.

Téllez, M. "Heat Death of Western Human Arrogance." In *Meanwhile, Elsewhere: Science Fiction and Fantasy from Transgender Writers*, edited by Cat Fitzpatrick and Casey Plett, 253-259. New York: Topside Press, 2017.

Ueda, Sayuri. *The Cage of Zeus*. San Francisco: Haikasoru Books, 2011.

Varley, John. "Options." In *Universe 9*, edited by Terry Carr, 188-222. New York: Doubleday, 1979.

Wachowskis, The. *Sense8*. Netflix, 2015-2018. https://www.netflix.com/title/80025744.

Ward, Cynthia. "Body Drift." *Analog Science Fiction and Fact*, Vol. 138, No. 11-12, November 2018, 169-174.

Williams-Childs, Brendan. "Schwaberow, Ohio." In *Meanwhile, Elsewhere: Science Fiction and Fantasy from Transgender Writers*, edited by Cat Fitzpatrick and Casey Plett, 295-310. New York: Topside Press, 2017. [Also at: https://medium.com/@b.williamschilds/schwaberow-ohio-632236506132]

Wolfmoor, Merc Fenn. "The Frequency of Compassion." *Uncanny Magazine*, Disabled People Destroy Science Fiction, Sept-Oct 2018. https://uncannymagazine.com/article/the-frequency-of-compassion/.

—. "Trust in the Law, for the Law Trusts in You." In *The Dystopia Triptych: Ignorance Is Strength*, edited by John Joseph Adams, Christie Yant, and Hugh Howey. New

York: Broad Reach Publishing, 2020. http://www.johnjosephadams.com/series/the-dystopia-triptych/.

—. "Believe in the Law, For the Law Is All." In *The Dystopia Triptych: Burn the Ashes*, edited by John Joseph Adams, Christie Yant, and Hugh Howey. New York: Broad Reach Publishing, 2020. http://www.johnjosephadams.com/series/the-dystopia-triptych/.

—. "The Law Is the Plan, and the Plan Is Death." In *The Dystopia Triptych: Or Else the Light*, edited by John Joseph Adams, Christie Yant, and Hugh Howey. New York: Broad Reach Publishing, 2020. http://www.johnjosephadams.com/series/the-dystopia-triptych/.

Secondary Works Cited

4 Non Blondes. "What's Up." *Bigger, Better, Faster, More.* Interscope Records, 1992.

"About Us." *Robot Companion,* 2021, https://www.robotcompanion.ai/about-us/.

Bernard, Katie and Sydney Hoover. "KS Senate Approves Bill Barring Transgender Students from Participating in Girls Sports." *The Kansas City Star,* 17 March 2021. https://www.kansascity.com/news/politics-government/article250016854.html.

Bigelow, John. "Time Travel Fiction." In *Reality and Humean Supervenience: Essays on the Philosophy of David Lewis,* edited by Gerhard Preyer and Frank Siebelt, 57-92. Lanham, MD: Rowman and Littlefield, 2001.

"Black Girl Magic." *Wikipedia,* 2021. https://en.wikipedia.org/wiki/Black_Girl_Magic.

Bordo, Susan. "'Material Girl': The Effacements of Postmodern Culture." In *The Female Body: Figures, Styles, Speculations,* edited by Laurence Goldstein, 106-130. Ann Arbor: The University of Michigan Press, 1991.

"Bordo, Susan." *Wikipedia,* https://en.wikipedia.org/wiki/Susan_Bordo.

Borges, Jorge Luis. "The Library of Babel." In *Ficciones,* 112-118. New York: Grove Press, 1962.

Bornstein, Kate. *Gender Outlaw: On Men, Women, and the Rest of Us.* New York: Vintage, 1995.

Buchanan, A. C. "Editorial." *Capricious Magazine,* Gender Diverse Pronouns Issue, Iss. 9, January 2018.

Works Cited

Butler, Judith. *Gender Trouble: Feminism and the Subversion of Identity*. New York: Routledge, 1989.

Čapek, Karel. *R.U.R. (Rossum's Universal Robots)*, Trans. Claudia Novack. New York: Penguin, 2004 (1921).

Carter, Raphael. "Not This, Not That." *Androgyny RAQ (Rarely Asked Questions)*, 21 March 1988. https://web.archive.org/web/20000815073625/http://www.chaparraltree.com/raq/.

Cipri, Nino. "The Accidental Organizer—Or, How I Lost One Job, Helped Unionize Another, and Managed to Survive." *Nino Cipri*, 17 September 2017. https://ninocipri.com/2015/09/17/the-accidental-organizer-or-how-i-lost-one-job-helped-unionize-another-and-managed-to-survive/.

—. "Nino Cipri | Finna." *Fresh Fiction*, 5 March 2020. https://blog.freshfiction.com/nino-cipri-finna/

Combahee River Collective, The. "The Combahee River Collective Statement." *BlackPast*. https://www.blackpast.org/african-american-history/combahee-river-collective-statement-1977/.

Coogler, Ryan. *Black Panther*. Walt Disney Studios, 2018.

Crenshaw, Kimberlé. "Demarginalizing the Intersection of Race and Sex: A Black Feminist Critique of Antidiscrimination Doctrine, Feminist Theory, and Antiracist Politics." *The University of Chicago Legal Forum*, Vol. 1989, Article 8. https://chicagounbound.uchicago.edu/uclf/vol1989/iss1/8/.

Dattaro, Laura. "Largest Study to Date Confirms Overlap between Autism and Gender Diversity." *Spectrum*, 14 September 2020. https://www.spectrumnews.org/news/largest-study-to-date-confirms-overlap-between-autism-and-gender-diversity/.

De Beauvoir, Simone. *Le duxième sexe*. Paris: Gallimard, 1949.

Del Rey, Lester. "War of the Sexes." *Analog: Science Fiction, Science Fact*, 95, 6, June 1975, 166-170.

Delany, Samuel R. *The Motion of Light in Water: Sex and Science Fiction Writing in the East Village, 1957-1965*. New York: Arbor House, 1988.

—. "The Semiology of Silence." *Science Fiction Studies* 14, Iss. 2 (1987). https://www.depauw.edu/sfs/interviews/delany42interview.htm.

Dery, Mark. "Black to the Future: Interviews with Samuel R. Delany, Greg Tate, and Tricia Rose." *The South Atlantic Quarterly* 92, Iss. 4 (1993): 735-778.

Disturbed. "The Sound of Silence." *YouTube*, 8 December 2015. https://www.youtube.com/watch?v=u9Dg-g7t2l4.

Dorsey, Candace Jane. "Some Notes on the Failure of Sex and Gender Inquiry in SF." *Science Fiction Studies* 3, Iss. 36, SFS Symposium: Sexuality in Science Fiction, (2009): 389-390.

Ellison, Harlan. *Dangerous Visions*. New York: Signet, 1967.

—. *Again, Dangerous Visions*. New York: Doubleday, 1972.

Fausto-Sterling, Anne. "The Five Sexes: Why Male and Female Are Not Enough." *The Sciences*, 33, 2, 1993, 20-24.

Fem the Future, 2021. http://www.femfuture.com/.

Ferry, Bryan. "In Every Dream Home a Heartache." *YouTube*, 15 August 2008. https://www.youtube.com/watch?v=LSniBxXjK_8.

Friedan, Betty. *The Feminine Mystique*. New York: W. W. Norton Company, 1963.

Frye, Marilyn. "Oppression." *Feminist Frontiers*, 6th ed., edited by Laurel Richardson, Verta A. Taylor, and Nancy Whittier, 84-90. Boston: McGraw-Hill, 2004.

Gass, William. "Philosophy and the Future of Fiction." *Syracuse Scholar* (1979-1991) 1, Iss. 2, (1980): 1-13. https://surface.syr.edu/suscholar/vol1/iss2/3.

Genesis. "The Cinema Show." *Selling England by the Pound*. Charisma, 1973.

—. "The Fountain of Salmacis." *Nursery Cryme*. Charisma, 1971.

—. "Heathaze." *Duke*. Charisma, 1980.

Gidney, Craig. "Tanith Lee: Channeling Queer Authors." *Lambda Literary*, 13 September 2011. https://www.lambdaliterary.org/interviews/09/13/tanith-lee-queer-authors/.

Harter, Richard. "Science Fiction Is Trash." *Richard Harter's World*, 26 Feb. 1998. https://richardhartersworld.com/trash-2/.

Haver, William. "Queer Research, or, How to Practise Invention to the Brink of Unintelligibility." In *The Eight Technologies of Otherness*, edited by Sue Golding, 277-292. London: Routledge, 1997.

Heinlein, Robert A. *Podkayne of Mars*. New York: G. P. Putnam's Sons, 1963.

Hoard, Christian. "Artist of the Week: Janelle Monáe." *Rolling Stone* 30 June 2010. https://www.rollingstone.com/music/music-news/artist-of-the-week-janelle-monae-186564/.

Hollinger, Veronica. "(Re)Reading Queerly: Science Fiction, Feminism, and the Defamiliarization of Gender." *Science Fiction Studies* 26, Iss. 1 (1999): 23-40.

"Interactive Kansas Seal." *Archive.org*, 2008. https://web.archive.org/web/20080704170629/http://governor.ks.gov/Facts/KansasSealInteractive.htm.

Jorgensen, Christine (1967). *Christine Jorgensen: A Personal Autobiography*. New York: Bantam Books.

"Jorgensen, Christine." Wikipedia. Last modified October 9, 2021. https://en.wikipedia.org/wiki/Christine_Jorgensen.

Kafka, Franz. *Metamorphosis*. London: Penguin Classics, 2016.

"Kansas State Motto." *Netstate.com*, 25 February 2016. https://www.netstate.com/states/mottoes/ks_motto.htm.

"Kansas' Equality Profile." *Movement Advancement Project*, 2021. https://www.lgbtmap.org/equality_maps/profile_state/KS.

King, Martin Luther. "I Have a Dream." Speech presented at the March on Washington for Jobs and Freedom, Washington, D.C., August 1968. https://avalon.law.yale.edu/20th_century.

Labonté, Richard and Lawrence Schimel. *The Future Is Queer*, Vancouver, BC: Arsenal Press, 2006.

Le Guin, Ursula. "Myth and Archetype in Science Fiction." In *The Language of the Night*, 73-81. New York, Berkeley, 1985.

The Ling Space, YouTube. https://www.youtube.com/channel/UCdZcGRaBV-VRRyU4t6Ur0mw.

lloyd, emily. "'This Bridge Called My Mac.'" Lesbian Feminist Politics on the Internet." *Off Our Backs* 25, Iss. 1 (1995): 12-13.

Works Cited

Lorde, Audre. "Age, Race, Class and Sex: Women Redefining Difference." In *Sister Outsider*, 114-123. Berkeley, CA: Crossing Press, 1984.

—. "Artisan." In *The Collected Poems of Audre Lorde*, 301. New York: W. W. Norton Company, 1997.

Lothian, Alexis. *Old Futures: Speculative Fiction and Queer Possibility*. New York: New York University Press, 2018.

MacNaron, Toni A. H. *Poisoned Ivy: Lesbian and Gay Academics Confronting Homophobia*. Philadelphia: Temple University Press, 1997.

Mandelo, Lee. "Queering SFF: 12 Authors, Critics, and Activists on What's Changed in the Last Ten Years." *Tor.com*, 31 March 2020, https://www.tor.com/2020/03/31/queering-sff-12-authors-critics-and-activists-on-whats-changed-in-the-last-ten-years/.

—. "Tanith Lee: A Brief Retrospective." *Tor.com*, 29 May, 2015. https://www.tor.com/2015/05/29/tanith-lee-a-brief-retrospective/.

McGuire, Barry. "The Eve of Destruction." *YouTube*, 15 August 2017. https://www.youtube.com/watch?v=MdWGp3HQVjU.

McNeil, Kevin. "Author Spotlight: Nino Cipri." *Nightmare Magazine*, Iss. 63, December 2017. http://www.nightmare-magazine.com/nonfiction/author-spotlight-nino-cipri/.

"The Metamorphosis." *Wikipedia*, 2 June 2021. https://en.wikipedia.org/wiki/The_Metamorphosis.

Morgan, Cheryl. "Joanna Russ." *Cheryl's Mewsings*, 1 May 2011. https://www.cheryl-morgan.com/?p=10581.

Mullen, R. D. "The Gregg Press Science Fiction Series (Continued)." *Science Fiction Studies* 5, no. 2 (1978): 192-196. https://www.depauw.edu/sfs/birs/bir15.htm#D1.

Murphy, Jennifer et al. "Autism and Transgender Identity: Implications for Depression and Anxiety." *Research in Autism Spectrum Disorders*, Vol. 69, January 2020. https://www.sciencedirect.com/science/article/pii/S1750946719301540.

Newton, Esther. *Mother Camp: Female Impersonators in America*. Chicago: Chicago University Press, 1979.

Newton, Huey. "War Poster." *Penn State University Libraries*, Digital Collections, 1967. https://digital.libraries.psu.edu/digital/collection/warposters/id/269/.

Ovid. *Metamorphoses, Project Gutenberg*, 2007. https://www.gutenberg.org/files/21765/21765-h/21765-h.htm.

Panshin, Alexei and Cory. "Books." *The Magazine of Fantasy and Science Fiction*, 49.2, August 1975, 46-53.

Pearson, Wendy Gay. "Alien Cryptographies." *Science Fiction Studies*, Vol. 26, No. 1 (1999): 1-22.

Perry, Donna. "Joanna Russ." In *Backtalk: Women Writers Speak Out*, 287-311. New Brunswick, NJ: Rutgers University Press, 1993.

"Pussy Riot." *YouTube*, 2021. https://www.youtube.com/user/PussyRiotOfficial.

RealDoll. 2021, https://www.realdoll.com.

Redding-Gonzalez, KC. "Tanith Lee: Why Was One of Horror's Best Female Writers Blacklisted? A Women in Horror Month Tribute, Part 1." *Zombie Salmon (The Horror Continues)*, 1 February 2019. https://zombiesalmonthehorrorcontinues.wordpress.com/tag/where-is-tanith-lee/.

Works Cited

Rimbaud, Arthur and Martin Sorrell. "Le bâteau ivre." In *Collected Poems*, 124-129. Oxford: Oxford University Press, 2001.

"R.U.R." *Wikipedia*, 24 May 2021. https://en.wikipedia.org/wiki/R.U.R.

Russ, Joanna. "Recent Feminist Utopias." In *To Write Like a Woman: Essays in Feminism and Science Fiction*, 133-148. Bloomington, IN: Indiana University Press, 1995.

Sandifer, Elizabeth. "A Short Guide to Janelle Monáe and the Metropolis Saga." *Eruditorium*, 30 June 2015. https://www.eruditorumpress.com/blog/a-short-guide-to-janelle-mone-and-the-metropolis-saga.

Scott, Melissa. *Shadow Man*. New York: Tor, 1995.

Shakespeare, William. "Hamlet." In *The Complete Works of Shakespeare*, 3rd edition, edited by David Bevington, 1091-1149. Glenview, IL: Scott, Foresman, and Company, 1980.

Shawl, Nisi, Cynthia Ward, and K. Tempest Bradford. *Writing the Other*, 2021. https://writingtheother.com/.

Silverberg, Robert. *The Lost Races of Mars*. New York: John C. Winston, 1960.

Simon, Paul and Art Garfunkel. "The Sound of Silence." *YouTube*, 19 May 2017. https://www.youtube.com/watch?v=nwP3vPQi0nI.

Sjunneson, Elsa and Dominik Parisien. "The *Disabled People Destroy Science Fiction* Manifesto." *Uncanny*, 2018. https://uncannymagazine.com/article/the-disabled-people-destroy-science-fiction-manifesto/.

Stone, Sandy. "Will the Real Body Please Stand Up?" *Semantic Scholar*, 1994. https://pdfs.semanticscholar.

org/15c5/9cbd90e808314fbfe7952127bf9f5f31c6b2. pdf+&cd=1&hl=en&ct=clnk&gl=us.

Téllez, M. *Cyborg Memoirs*. https://cyborgmemoirs. com/2016/07/heat-death-of-western-human-arrogance/.

Tiptree, James, Jr., "Love Is the Plan, the Plan Is Death." In *Warm Worlds and Otherwise*, 173-193. New York: Ballantine, 1975.

—. "The Women Men Don't See." In *Warm Worlds and Otherwise*, 131-164. New York: Del Rey, 1975.

"TMM Update Trans Day of Remembrance 2019." *Transrespect versus Transphobia*, 11 November 2019. https://transrespect.org/en/tmm-update-trans-day-of-remembrance-2019/.

Vilain, Eric, et al. "We Used to Call Them Hermaphrodites." *Genetics in Medicine*, Vol. 9, February 2007. https://www.nature.com/articles/gim200711.

"Weeks, Jeffrey." *Wikipedia*, https://en.wikipedia.org/wiki/Jeffrey_Weeks_(sociologist).

Weeks, Jeffrey, *Sexuality*. London, New York: E. Horwood, Tavistock Publications, 1986.

Winnington. "I Sexually Identify As an Attack Helicopter." *Know Your Meme*, 2015. https://knowyourmeme.com/memes/i-sexually-identify-as-an-attack-helicopter.

Yeats, W. B. "A Coat." *The Collected Poems of W. B. Yeats*, 142. New York: Macmillan, 1956.

Zoline, Pamela. "The Heat Death of the Universe." In *Women of Wonder: The Contemporary Years*, edited by Pamela Sargent, 205-217. San Diego: Harvest Books, 1995.

About the Author

Ritch Calvin (he/him) was born and raised in a small farming town in northwest Ohio. Don't let the picture books fool you. It wasn't all that bucolic. Science fiction was a way out. After he had exhausted the entire SF collection at the local library, he discovered (his mother was a librarian) the wonders of interlibrary loan. Although he spent many years working in a local factory, he also co-owned and ran a bookstore. While listening to a shortwave radio in that bookstore, he heard an interview with Carlos Fuentes, and that opened up a whole other world.

He obtained a BA and MA in English from Bowling Green State University and a PhD in Comparative Literature from SUNY Stony Brook. He is now an Associate Professor of Women's, Gender, and Sexuality Studies.

He served on the Executive Committee of the Science Fiction Research Association (SFRA) for six years (two as VP, two as President, and two as Past President). He was also the media reviews editor for the SFRA Review for six years. He was the Conference Director for the SFRA's 2015 annual conference (Vandana Singh, Alexis Lothian, and M. Asli Dukan were the Guests of Honor).

He has published essays in *Extrapolation, Femspec, Science Fiction Film and Television, Science Fiction Studies, New York Review of Science Fiction,* and *SFRA Review.* His bibliography of the works of Octavia E. Butler appeared in *Utopian Studies* in 2008. His first edited collection, on Gilmore Girls, appeared in 2007. In 2014, he edited (with Doug Davis, Karen Hellekson, and Craig Jacobsen) a volume of essays entitled *SF 101: An Introduction to Teaching and Studying Science Fiction.* In 2016, he published *Feminist Epistemology and Feminist Science Fiction: Four Modes* (Palgrave). He is currently working on a book on short science fiction film (with Paweł Frelik) and a book on C. J. Cherryh.